POPULATION

K. A. GANDY

THIGPEN-
GANDY
PUBLISHING

THIGPEN-GANDY PUBLISHING

For my Dad, who raised me to fiercely believe that I could do anything, be anything, and achieve anything.

Turns out, you were right.

This one's for you, Dad.

CONTENTS

ONE

TWO TICKETS TO PARADISE

The sun peeks through my window so bright and cheerful, it seems like any other day. As if today the only thing that will happen is the sun beaming down on flat pastures, the wind blowing through the pine trees, and the horses and cows grazing lazily. If only it was still yesterday. I know they say you can't live in the past, but yesterday was my last day of freedom. At least for a few years, possibly ever. It's going to be hard to let go of that day and embrace this one.

With a stretch, I climb out of bed and start to dress for what's coming. But what do you wear for the day your life is no longer your own? Well, I'm going with jeans. They are my protective armor. Jeans, my favorite boots, and a tank top are a little piece of comfort, and they let me pretend a while longer that all I'll be doing today is going out to saddle up and hit the woods with some of my brothers. Maybe check fences, or move some cows. But then, if that was my today, my wheeled duffle wouldn't be sitting stuffed by my bedroom door. I pick up my pillow and shove it through the carry handle of my bag. There's no use pretending when I've known for three years now the fate that awaits me, awaits every woman in the North American Alliance.

I've known since I turned sixteen that a shuttle would be waiting in town today, to take me to the New Life Center of Georada. Somehow it still feels surreal, impossible. Is this really it? I mean, they send you a brochure on your sixteenth birthday, all glossy and freshly pressed, with pictures of happy, smiling women and handsome men with jaws that could cut glass. Little blurbs about how they will match you with your very own prince charming, your perfect genetic other half, and then send you off to a honeymoon paradise for the first two years of your new life together. Two years, or until I'm pregnant; whichever comes first.

My heart nearly broke telling Morgan goodbye yesterday. We went on a long, leisurely trail ride, just me and him. When we got back, I untacked him, and gave him the best brushing down of his life. Somewhere in the middle the tears started to flow, until all I could do was cling to his big, warm neck and cry into his mane. There aren't words to describe how much I will miss him, even though I know my family will treat him like a king. Mom's going to do her best to fatten him up by feeding him leftover biscuits; I won't be here to stop her.

After getting ready in the bathroom, I pull out the handle on my bag with a click and wheel it down the hallway to the kitchen. Being the youngest of seven is no walk in the park, especially if you're the only girl. But, I love my brothers. I would not trade having a single one for more girl time, or another stolen kiss with a boy in the hay loft. We are close, and the thought of telling them all goodbye today is tearing me in two. Gavin is already in the kitchen nursing a cup of coffee.

"Good morning squirt," he says with a sad grin. He'd usually be out in the back pastures by now, so I know he's here to say his goodbyes. "How are you today? Hanging in there? I see you didn't get all dolled up for the bus of doom."

I laugh, "If the bus of doom doesn't like me as I am, I guess it'll just have to send me back." That'd just be too dang bad, wouldn't it? 'Sorry, ma'am, you don't have glossy, shiny brochure-lady vibes, so please return to your ranch immediately.' I am so not that lucky. He reaches back to the counter, and hands me a mug, which I can see marshmallows floating in. He's pulling out all the stops today, hot chocolate with marshmallows before breakfast. I take a grateful sip, and give him a side hug. We hang like that for a few moments, just soaking up the early morning quiet, until we hear boots on the porch and the screen door bangs open.

"Sadie! Where are you?" Brent hollers. That man is always loud.

"In the kitchen, and quit yelling, it's way too early for that," I answer.

"Who's yelling?" he yells again, as Phil and Cade walk in behind him. Cade walks straight over and wraps me in a bear hug, lifting my feet off the ground in the process. I shove my mug out to the side so it doesn't spill, and set it back on the counter before hugging him back. Once he puts me down, I see they are all in their work clothes, well-worn jeans with leather gloves hanging out of back pockets. They've probably been out mending fences and checking the herds since dawn. It's getting close to time to start thinning the herds before winter, and they'll be busy the next few weeks sorting them and bringing in the ones for the sale, and moving the rest of the herd out to the winter pastures. Only, I won't be here this year.

"How are the cows looking?" I ask, making small talk while they grab their own cups of coffee.

"They're doing fine, Sadie." Phil answers, giving me a peck on the cheek and handing back my mug. "How are you holding up?" he asks with concern. Phil, the quiet sincere one. He doesn't say a whole lot, but he's all heart. That's how he scooped Tess up so quickly; he and his high school sweetheart live across the way with their two sons. She passed on her blonde hair and blue eyes to both of my adorable nephews.

"I'm okay, just trying not to think about it." I refuse to start this new phase of my life with a tear-stained face. Just because it feels more like I'm heading to hell than paradise, doesn't mean I'm not going to face it head on. They can print all the shiny happy photos of the New Life Center they want, that doesn't change the fact that I have no choice but to participate in the compulsory marriage program.

Marriage, at nineteen. I'm not ready to give up my freedom, but for women nowadays that's merely a childhood illusion. It's been years since any woman was actually free to choose her own fate. My parents were one of the last generations where participation was optional. We're the rarity now. Most families have zero to one child, two if they're extremely lucky. So, the North American Alliance created the New Lives Program, to help people find a better genetic match. People praised it as an amazing humanitarian effort at first, when it was voluntary. All the reports showed a thirty percent higher birth rate among couples who found their genetic match at a New Life Center.

It wasn't enough, though. Population rates are still in decline, and one day they dipped below an "acceptable level" to sustain even our new, pared down society. So here I am, nineteen. Three years after my glossy brochure promised me a perfect genetic match, and, you know, maybe someone I could grow to love . . . saying goodbye to my family, to go be a trumped-up broodmare with every other woman of age on the continent.

I look around at my four brothers and try not to break my "no tears" resolve. With Peter off in the NAA Police Force and

Teddy in training to join, the five of us are the only ones left at home. After today, our seven will be whittled down to four.

"Mom and Dad should be here any minute with your breakfast for the road," Brent says, breaking into my distracted state. "I hear Mom's making you the full works; I think she's worried you're going to forget home cooking before they let you come back." He says with a wry grin. As if *anyone* could forget my mother's cooking.

As if on cue, a familiar pattern is rapped on the front door. "I hope everybody's decent in there!" my dad hollers, as he lets himself and my mom in.

"We've been up for nearly two hours, Dad." Gavin huffs, "Besides, you know Sadie doesn't tolerate shenanigans in the bunk house." He reaches over and grabs the basket Mom's carrying, covered in a blue gingham towel, and then reaches down to pick up my suitcase. He heads toward the front door, to load both things in the truck.

Mom responds, "It's a good thing—somebody has to keep you knuckleheads in line. What are we going to do without our sweet Sadie?" She's trying and failing not to choke up. I walk over and give both my parents a hug.

"I'm sure they'll be fine, Mom. They were fine on their own before, and they'll be fine while I'm gone." She brushes my hair out of my face and lays her hand on my cheek. Her gentle touch has been honed by years of rocking babies and kissing skinned knees, and I will miss her with every fiber of my being.

"I know they will sweetheart, we're just all going to miss you. I hate that instead of a fairy tale, you're getting an arranged marriage. This is not what we ever wanted for you. But I am praying that you find your perfect match, even if it's under less-than-ideal circumstances."

Dad cuts in, "She'll be okay, darlin'. If there's one thing our Sadie is, it's tough; and she's too smart to fall for anybody who doesn't deserve her. Isn't that right, Sadie-bear?" He wraps his arm tightly around Mom's waist, and my heart squeezes in my chest at the familiar sight.

I smile back weakly, "You're right, Dad. I'll pick a good son-in-law for you, don't worry." I am worried, though. Once my testing is complete, I'll be set up with my best genetic matches. And if there's only one? There's only one, and I'll be walking down the aisle with him, whoever he is.

Gavin comes back in, screen door slamming shut behind him. He doesn't say anything, but he doesn't have to. He just waits, hands in his pockets. This is it, it's time to head to town, where the bus of doom awaits. I give everyone one last hug, and head out the front door to the truck. Gavin slides into the worn-out driver's seat of the farm truck and cranks it up, while Cade walks me to the passenger side and opens the door for me, ever the gentleman.

"Stay safe, baby sister," he says as I climb in.

I give him my strongest smile, "Love you big brother, I'll be back before you know it." He smiles back and shuts the door carefully. Head tucked low and hands in his pockets, he walks back towards the others standing on the porch. We'd had a farewell dinner last night, and stayed up until the wee hours packed into my parents' kitchen, telling stories and laughing. We'd hugged and shared our favorite memories until we couldn't keep our eyes open. I didn't want a big public goodbye at the shuttle station, despite my parents' protests. There's no way I'd get on the bus, if they were all standing there comforting Mom while she cried.

Gavin pulls out of the drive, and we bump along toward the main road. I look out the window just before the turn, and give them a final, melancholy wave. They all wave in return, except Mom, whose head is already buried in Dad's shoulder. My heart clenches at the sight.

The truck is quiet with both of us focused on munching on Mom's homemade biscuit sandwiches, so I reach over and turn on the radio. The NAA One announcer says they're doing an oldies hour and I have to laugh at what starts playing. Two Tickets to Paradise blasts through the speakers.

Somehow, I don't think government-arranged marriage is what Eddie Money had in mind when he wrote this song two hundred years ago.

TWO

BUS OF DOOM

The ride to town is uneventful, and a little while later we pull up in front of town hall. Gavin throws the truck in park, but leaves his hand tense on the gear shifter. "Sadie, I—" he pauses, clears his throat, "I want you to know that we are here for you, however this ends. Whenever this ends. You may not have a choice in this, but we will always choose you, no matter what." He starts to choke up, and I try to cut him off.

"Gavin, please don't cry. I'll be back. Things won't be the same, but I'll be back one day, hopefully sooner than later." If he cries, I'll start and won't be able to stop, and I don't want to see my immovable big brother brought to tears over me. I don't want that to be the last interaction between us for the next two years.

"Let me finish. You know that little spot near the side forty, with the giant oak and all the wildflowers each summer?" he asks.

"Yeah. Of course I know it, Morgan and I have spent countless afternoons reading under that tree when it's hot as Hades out."

"Well, we had a family meeting, and we all agreed. That spot is yours. And when you get home, you're going to have a brand new home, right there. The boys and I are going to build it for

8

you and your future family. We're going to make it real pretty for you, with a huge stone fireplace, and a little window seat that looks out over a pasture for Morgan. We went through your sketchbook and got some good ideas." He smiles with a small quirk of his mouth, nothing huge, just enough to show that he's hopeful but also worried I won't like the idea. He's wrong. I love the idea.

I throw myself across the center console and hug him hard. "That sounds perfect, Gavin. Really, really perfect. Now I'm going to be dying to come back even sooner, to see what you guys do." Now I'm the one choking up. *Dang it, reel it in Sadie!* "You are the best big brother I could ask for, Gavin. I'm going to miss you guys every day. Promise you won't forget me?"

"Aww, Sadie-bear, we couldn't forget you any more than we could forget the sun itself. You're going to be fine. Just make sure whoever you pick knows he's got six of us to answer to, so he better treat you right. Or he just might meet Peter in a dark alley." He's suddenly serious, "I don't care what this program claims—if he doesn't treat you well, there will be consequences, do you hear me?"

"I hear you, I hear you. I'd never allow someone like that within ten feet of me. Y'all taught me better." *Assuming I have more than one choice, that is.* We say our final goodbyes as the shuttle pulls in. It's sleek, and huge. The exterior is wrapped with a silver banner that screams, "Your New Life Awaits!" If only a new life was what I was after.

There are several other girls milling around, a few I know, but surprisingly a few I don't, as well. It looks like there are about seven of us catching this shuttle to the capital city. I give a small wave to the four girls I recognize from school, and they wave back with varying degrees of excitement as they say goodbye to their families. The younger the girl, the bigger the wave. It seems they've bought into the idea of wedded bliss and a two year vacation in paradise a bit more than I have—and by how young they look, a few of them must have had their parents sign the waiver to come a year early, at sixteen. Not me. I loved my life too much to want to leave a second sooner than I had to.

Off the shuttle steps a man who looks to be in his early forties, with movie-star good looks. He's clean shaven, and wearing a blazer over a button up shirt. He takes us all in and smiles, and his teeth could be in a toothpaste commercial, they're so white. "Welcome ladies! My name is Eric, and I'll be your escort to the Georada New Life Center! I hope you're all as excited to be here as we are to have you! If you'd all line up with your bags, I'll be checking you in, and Todd, our driver, will be loading your bags under the shuttle for you." Todd steps out of the shuttle and gives us a cursory wave before popping open the luggage compartment of the shuttle.

"Once everyone is present and accounted for, you'll all be able to choose your seats and we'll get on the road. You'll find everything you need inside; we have a full restroom, snacks, and beverages. As well as on-board entertainment. If you ladies find you need anything that we haven't anticipated, I'll be right here with you the whole way; all you have to do is ask. Every one of your heart's desires is safe with me." He finishes with a twinkle in his eye and a hand over his heart.

The girls start giving final hugs and lining up, a single bag in tow for each of them. I turn to Gavin, who's trying and failing to hide a mildly disgusted look. "He's really laying it on thick, huh? 'Your heart's desire', really? How much do you think they pay him to say that?"

"Gavin, I'm sure he's just trying to make everyone feel comfortable. What's he supposed to say, 'Beware all who board this bus of doom?'"

He chuckles and loosens his stranglehold on my bag, "Fine, fine. I'm just not buying it, is all I'm saying." He leans over and gives me a swift kiss to the forehead, and then reluctantly hands me my bag. "I'm going to wait right here until you're safely off. As soon as they'll let you, you call us. Or write us, or both, okay? There's nothing too big or too small to tell us. And stay away from Eric; he gives me a bad vibe."

"I know Gav, I know. I'll write as much as I can. You'll be sick of hearing from me, promise." I pause. I guess this is really it. "Take really good care of Morgan for me, okay? Show him my picture, and make sure he gets ridden a few times a week. Try to make sure Mom doesn't just fatten him up with biscuits and apples. It's really not good for a horse to have that much bread."

"Promise, little sister. Now get over there. The sooner you get going, the sooner you get back." And just like that, I'm turning my back on my family and getting in the first line of my new life.

By the time I make it there, there is only one girl left ahead of me, and one girl ahead of her handing Todd her very hefty suitcase. The girl directly in front of me is one I recognize barely, she's a few years younger than me. She looks barely sixteen, and she's rubbing one arm whether with nerves or cold, I can't tell.

"Name?" Eric asks her.

"Nell," she says, "Nell Jones, from West Georada."

"Welcome, Nell! I see you've had quite a trek already this morning, but hopefully things will be comfortable for you inside. If you'll just sign here, Todd is ready to take your bag." He passes her the tablet, where she hastily signs her initials. She then walks toward Todd, and hands him her backpack. I'd noticed her standing alone earlier; maybe her family couldn't travel with her from so far away.

"Traveling light, huh?" Todd says affably as he takes the small bag and crams it in on top of the monster suitcase he'd just loaded. She nods to him without comment and makes her way to the stairs.

"Miss?" I jolt, and realize Eric has clearly been waiting on me, as I've been watching Nell board the shuttle.

"Sorry! I'm Sadie Taylor, I'm from right here in Jackson Flats," I answer quickly.

"Well miss Sadie Taylor, we're pleased to have you here with us today. Please give us your signature right here," he taps the tablet with precision, and then hands it to me, "and we'll be on our way shortly. It looks like we have one more straggler to wait for, before we can hit the road."

I quickly scrawl my name with my finger, and pass the device back to him. He gives me a smile and nods his head in Todd's direction, clearly ready for me to get a move on. I walk over, and pass Todd the handle to my bag, which he clicks down and loads. "Thanks, ma'am. Head right on in. If you need anything, just give one of us a holler."

"Thanks, Todd. I will," Todd seems to be your typical blue-collar guy, simply happy to be gainfully employed and none too impressed with the whole situation. This is probably par for the course for him. I can't imagine how many young women he's ferried off to new lives. I *wonder how many of them are happier than they were before they climbed on Todd's shuttle?* I make my way up the few steps, and I have to admit, they've gone all out on this setup.

The shuttle only seats ten passengers—with five plush recliners down each side of a center aisle— plus places for Eric and Todd. Each recliner is its own station, with a small console attached to the floor next to it. The first six recliners are taken, so I make my way to the middle of the bus, and slide into the recliner just behind Nell, who's perched at the edge of her seat, looking uncomfortable. I reach over and pop open my console, to see that there is an assortment of snacks and bottled drinks, as well as a pull out drawer equipped with fluffy slippers, a silky eye mask, headphones, and even a small collection of lip balm and other make-up items. It seems they really have tried to think of everything.

The bus windows are tinted from the outside, but from inside the view is crystal clear, and I spot Gavin, true to his word, still leaning against the hood of the truck. His poker face is back in place, and for all anyone would know he is just waiting for a bus himself. Then I spot movement from the corner of my eye, towards the far end of the parking lot. Oh, no. It's Beth-Ann and Phil. This is not going to go well. I am shocked that she's here today, since she swore she would wait until the last possible minute, like me. She has another six months until she turns nineteen, so I have no idea why she's here today.

Beth-Ann and Phil are clinging to each other, kissing without regard for who is watching, despite the larger-than-life shuttle and waiting escorts. They pull apart, Beth-Ann visibly sobbing, before she flings herself back into his arms. He holds her tightly, eyes closed for a moment, before gently holding her back by her shoulders. It's impossible to tell what they're saying from here, but it's clearly tense. He gives her one last chaste kiss on the forehead, and she stumbles back a step before grabbing her bag from where it was forgotten on the pavement. She slowly makes her way to where Eric is standing outside the shuttle, clearly impatient.

After the sign-in process, Beth-Ann's curly hair appears above the handrail a second before she does, face blotchy and red from crying. She's still sniffling quietly but trying to pull it together. Scanning the rows, her eyes lock with mine, and she quickly makes her way back to the seat across from mine, behind massive-suitcase girl, who's already kicked back with her silk eye mask in place, and headphones on.

"Sadie! I'm so glad you're here! This would have been a million times worse if I didn't know anyone!" Beth-Ann says, a catch in her voice.

"I'm glad to see you too, Beth-Ann, but I thought you had six more months? What happened? Why aren't you spending your last six months with Phil?" I ask.

She sniffles loudly, "Phil inherited his grandparents' house last week, when his grandfather passed. He, he—" she stops, unable to finish.

I lean across the aisle and grab her hands, "It's okay, Beth-Ann, slow down and just tell me what happened."

Taking a deep, ragged breath she continues, "He asked me to move in with him. He said he didn't care what happened, what husband I was matched with. He'd wait for me. Opt out of the program himself, work and save up here, and in three years when we're allowed to separate, he says he'll adopt my baby and we can go right back to how things were. He was willing to do that for me!" she says with a sob, "He didn't even care he'd be waiting alone for years and raising another man's child. He said he just wanted ME. Can you believe it?" She pauses, and I nod. Phil is old-fashioned like that. He meant it when he said he'd wait.

"So, what changed?" I prod, uncertain.

"Well, I went home and told my parents that I was moving out, that Phil and I were in love and we'd made a plan to make it work, despite the marriage mandate. They were completely shocked, and insisted I couldn't live with him unless we were allowed to marry. They said there are too many consequences if you're caught trying to work around the program. They said—"

"Breathe, Beth-Ann, just breathe a minute." I pat her hands. Her parents work for the city, so image is very important to them. But, surely not more important than the rest of Beth-Ann's life, right? She is their only daughter, surely they want to see her settled happily and close to home. There has to be some misunderstanding. I hear noise from the front of the bus, and realize Eric and Todd have closed up, and the bus doors have swung shut with a hiss. Eric has his own large recliner at the front, but his apparently also swivels to face us.

He sits down, swings around toward us, and clears his throat, "All right ladies, you eight are the full group this quarter. Once again, we're so pleased to have you here, and to help you get started with your bright new lives!" His gaze passes over us, lingering on Beth-Ann with a slight frown as he delivers the next part, "And we hope you'll all be as thrilled with your next chapters as we are to watch them unfold. Now, if you'll please fasten your seatbelts, we'll get on our way, finally. Does anyone need anything before Todd gets us going?" He pauses expectantly. "No? Okay then! The restrooms are in the back, feel free to use them at any time if you need to get cleaned up," his gaze settles on Nell, "or change your clothes, you'll find everything you need has been provided." With one last smile, he spins his chair forward, and signals Todd to pull out.

Todd has a drink in one hand, and the shifter in the other, as he smoothly starts us forward out of the parking lot and away from everything we know. I jerk around to look out and see Gavin still leaning against the hood of the truck. He's leaning forward just slightly now, and one hand is raised in a final wave. I know he can't see me through the tint, but I lean close to the glass and rest my hand against it anyway. I'm sure he knows I'm watching. I stay like that, as the shuttle pulls onto the road, and out of sight of the parking lot. A minute after it's completely out of sight, I lower my hand and lean back in my chair. I don't know for certain which is harder: being the one who goes or the one who's left. But I would give everything I own to be able to leap out of this shuttle and run straight back to my family's arms right now.

I forcibly close the door on that thought. I can't dwell on it, not today, not for a while. This is my new reality, and I have to keep my head clear for what's to come. My whole future is at stake in this program, and I have to choose wisely. My family is expecting it, expecting me to bring back a suitable husband, no matter what. Head back on straight, I turn back to Beth-Ann, and see that Nell is watching her also.

"Hello, Nell, was it?" I extend my hand, but she flinches back. She recovers quickly and shoves her hand out at mine.

"Yes, I'm Nell. And you are?" She sweeps her gaze to include Beth-Ann in the question.

"I'm Sadie, and this is Beth-Ann. It's a pleasure to meet you, although I do wish the circumstances were better." I say truthfully.

She shrugs, "They are what they are. At least this place is clean, and there are snacks," she says matter-of-factly.

"True, snacks make everything more tolerable." With that out of the way, Nell faces forward again, engrossing herself in a palm-sized device that she pulls from the console.

Dismissed, I turn sideways to continue my conversation with Beth-Ann, "So, your parents don't want you and Phil to wait for each other? They aren't okay with you coming back for him?"

More composed now, she shakes her head sadly, "No, they say he's unsuitable for the only daughter of the city hall's justice. You know I don't care that Phil's an ironworker, but apparently they've never liked him. All this time. Can you believe it?"

I'm not fully surprised, as I remember her parents disapproving when they'd first started dating three years back, but I assumed they'd grown to like him after all this time. Apparently, they'd just been biding their time for the program to do the dirty work of breaking their daughter's heart for them.

I shake my head, but try to stay positive, "Well, the good news is that it's not up to them. You're an adult, and they aren't in charge of what you do when you make it back from the program. You just have to get through this, and Phil will be waiting for you as planned."

She nods, "Well, the jokes on them. If they won't let us wait for each other, Phil's not going to opt out. He's signed up for the program, and we're going to try to get ourselves matched with each other. There's nothing they can do if we're a genetic match!"

"Phil's willing to do that? Even knowing he might get matched with another woman?" I'm shocked, as everyone in town knew he planned to opt out and continue his family's iron business.

At that, she finally smiles, "Yes, he's willing to do anything for me. He's it for me, Sadie, and I'm it for him." With a small sigh, she leans back in her chair, and I do the same.

I feel sorry for their circumstances, but deep down, I'm envious. It's not that I'm opposed to marriage and a family of my own, I've just never found "the one." When you've got parents like mine, settling for anything other than a lightning strike of attraction feels like asking for failure. I've been asked out a time or two, but never anyone I'd consider. I can't even imagine how I'd feel if I really had found the one, and still had to do this. Thank God for small blessings, I guess. Maybe I can still find him. My gaze flits back up to the front of the bus, and over the front window there is a screen which says ETA four hours, Atlanta New Life Center. Everyone else has pretty much settled in, so I head down the burnished wood aisle to the back of the bus to use the restroom. I choose the one on the right, and when the automatic light flicks on I am nearly blinded by all of the shiny bronze fixtures. I'll give them credit, they've really gone all out making this as nice of an experience as it can be. I quickly wash up, and head back to my seat. Maybe this won't be so awful; at least they're trying to make it nice. *Here's hoping.*

THREE

WELCOME TO THE DEEP END

T he drive to Atlanta is pretty uneventful. We stop for lunch at the designated waypoint. We older girls pick at our food, while the younger girls eat their tacos with excitement. I learn the rest of my shuttle-mates' names. Big suitcase girl is in fact Margaret, from South Georada. Her tanned skin, high-end clothes, and sun-bleached hair tell me she's from a beach town and a well-off family. She picks at a piece of brown-tinged lettuce at the edge of her salad bowl as if it's personally offended her, and feigns interest as Elena, one of my youngest classmates from Jackson Flats, chatters excitedly about what she read on her mini-tablet on the drive. Elena's brown skin tells of her family's Hispanic heritage. She's a sweet girl, and she's in love with the idea of love, as far as I can tell. She's spent the entire drive flipping through the Bachelor Book and reading up on all the men already in the eligibility pool for the compulsory marriage program.

At the other end of the table, Jenna and Leigh are discussing the coursework they left behind since they opted out of high school early. Charlotte sits at the end of the table between them, lost in her own thoughts. She is so quiet and reserved, I worry that this program is going to swallow her up. Hopefully she'll find herself and be okay. Beth-Ann is across from me, looking rather green around the gills. She hasn't touched her quesadilla, instead just taking delicate sips of a lemon soda.

"Bus ride not agreeing with you?" I ask her around a mouthful of enchilada. I'm never one to leave good food on the table, as ranch work takes a lot of energy.

She grimaces, "No, just not a big fan of greasy cheese," and then pushes the quesadilla across to me.

"It looks fine to me," I pick up a section and take a bite. "You're nuts, this is delicious!"

Margaret snorts, "Might want to take it easy there, Sadie. I know the men volunteered for this program, but that doesn't mean they want to be saddled with an overweight slob for a wife." She casts her eyes derisively down to where Charlotte is sitting.

I bristle. "Excuse me? Are you really going to take a jab at my eating when we only met a couple hours ago? Is that really how you want to start this?"

"I'm not here to impress any of you, and it's not my fault you can't handle the truth," she spits back without remorse.

"Well, maybe you should keep your ridiculous judgements to yourself. I'll eat what I want, and you can stay in your own lane." I look down the table at Charlotte, who has sunk down further in her seat. She's curvy, and I know she heard Margaret's stupid statement. Not that she was making any effort at discretion. "Besides, there's a lot more to beauty than being skinny. Personality and heart are worth a lot more than fitting into a tiny pair of jeans," I add for Charlotte's sake.

She rolls her eyes, "You keep telling yourself that." She gets up from the table and flounces off to the bathroom.

Beth-Ann snorts, "She's clearly not worried about making any friends on this trip."

"Clearly!" I agree wholeheartedly.

Once we're all back on the bus, Margaret immediately puts her eye mask and headphones back on and shuts us all out. The rest of us are more at ease with each other, courtesy of shared tacos. At the front of the bus, Jenna is trying to draw Charlotte into a conversation, but she still has that deflated air about her.

"All I'm saying is I'm pretty sure you'll get at least two to three matches, Charlotte. You have two siblings, right? That means you've got a great set of genes! I bet there will be plenty of genetic options for you to pick from. So, tell me, what's your type? Who's your favorite movie star?" Jenna probes.

Charlotte ponders the question carefully, and then answers, "Well, there are a lot of handsome men out there. Really any of them are fine, I just hope to find someone who listens when I talk, and cares about my point of view; I think that's important for a lasting relationship."

"Ugh," Jenna laments, "so we've got a true romantic on our hands here. Not me! I just want to get this thing over with. The sooner I'm matched and pop out a kid or two, the sooner I can move on with my life. I want to join the NAA Police Force, and do something cool. You know, maybe be a pilot, or an investigator! Something that matters."

"Hey! Being a mother matters," Leigh butts in. "If we don't have babies there won't be anyone to carry on the human race. That's about as *important* as it gets, don't you think? Motherhood is a true calling. I can't *wait* to be a mom. Think about it, if it weren't for this program, most of us would never be able to have a baby. "

"I'm not saying it isn't a calling, just that it's not my calling. My sperm donor can stay home with the kids while I go out and do something bigger in this world, that's all I'm saying." I can tell

Jenna is just getting fired up with this line of thought, but Eric clears his throat at the front of the shuttle.

"Ladies! Is everyone settled in and ready to finish today's journey? From what Todd tells me, we've only got an hour left before we arrive at the New Life Center. I've sent a short informational packet to each of your mini-tablets on what to expect during the intake process, so please take some time to review those before we arrive. If you have any questions, you know where to find me." With one last blinding smile, he turns back around and picks up his own tablet.

Oh goodie, intake process at the NLC. I can't wait to see what they plan to do with us next. I lean over and dig through the console at my side to find my assigned mini-tablet. Sure enough, there's an icon indicating I've got required reading assigned to me. I click it, and up pops an e-brochure.

Congratulations on taking your first steps on the journey to your new life! We are so happy to have you. Upon arrival at the New Life Center of Georada, you'll be escorted directly to our intake facility. The purpose of the intake facility is to start your baseline health file, which serves as the foundation of your care during your stay with us. We will immediately begin processing your genetic tests, so you can be matched to as many eligible bachelors as possible! Once your intake screening is complete, you will be added to our eligibility pool, and can receive matches from all over the North American Alliance; that's when the fun begins for our future mothers!

So sit back and enjoy the rest of your shuttle ride. You can get a head start on your health and history questionnaire below.

Once I finish reading the oh-so-informative blurb, it automatically pops up a questionnaire.

Name <u>Sadie Alice Taylor</u>

Age 19

Age of Mother 61

Age of Father 65

Number of Siblings 6

Oh heck, it wants details on every brother? I'm going to be at this the whole ride. After filling out all of the information including occupations, age, marital status, and number of children for every single brother, It finally tells me I'm done for now. Thank heavens. The device vibrates and I see it has another notification.

Congratulations on completing your preliminary intake questionnaire! Please enjoy flipping through our Bachelor Book while you wait to find your own perfect genetic matches!

I sigh. What is the point in looking at pictures of a bunch of men, most of whom I'll never meet? But yep, there it is; required reading. Cow crap. Sure, one of these guys is likely to be my husband in a few months, but shopping for one doesn't seem like a great plan for me, given the circumstances. What if I get my hopes up that there's some amazing guy in this book, and then I watch him get matched to Margaret? No, thanks. I'll just open it so it shows that I did it, and then exit straight out. *Deep breaths Sadie, it's just a book of dudes.*

I glance up and see we're now ten minutes out from our destination. Perfect! I won't have long to obsess over it. I click the link, and up pops the Bachelor Book App. The first page has three photos on it, and stats underneath for each man. Hi there, James, Marcus, and Devonte. They are all smiling, but that's where the similarities end. James is wearing a suit and red tie in his photo. Underneath it says he's twenty-seven, and is looking for a wife "who wants to stay home with their (hopefully three or more) kids, who loves to cook and keep house." His career is listed as "Assistant Justice of South Georada", so he's clearly interested in politics. His location is listed as fixed: South Georada Central. *Fixed? I wonder what that means.*

Marcus is wearing an NAA flight suit uniform, and his career is listed as an NAA pilot. I have to admit, he piques my interest. He looks handsome and strong in his uniform, and unlike James he's listed as looking for "A wife who wants to see the world and has a sense of adventure." No, this is dangerous. The likelihood of me getting genetically matched to Marcus is next to nil. Focus, Sadie. I switch to Devonte. He's handsome, too, with his dark, rich skin tone and friendly eyes. He's dressed casually, but neatly in his photo. His occupation is listed as "Business Owner" which is cool. Wants in a wife, "Someone who sees a baby as a blessing, like I do." Oh man, he'd be perfect for Charlotte. He's clearly got that romantic personality, and he looks kind. I tap the app closed.

I'm not sure if it's better or worse seeing these men as real humans with their own hopes and desires. On the one hand, it's better, because they're just people too. But on the other, it's worse because I could be a genetic match for someone who is completely wrong for me in every other way, and we would spend the next few years hating and disappointing each other. That sounds like hell on earth. I blow out a breath that pushes my bangs to the side and realize that the bus is pulling into a long, sloped driveway. This must be it, the NLC.

Todd pulls us straight up to the grand front entrance, and pops the doors open with a hiss. Eric stands, "Ok ladies! This is it, the Georada New Life Center. You're about to take the first steps into your bright futures. If you'll line up after me, I'll escort you directly to the Intake Room, where you'll be added to the eligibility pool!" He is all smiles, but I feel a sense of dread lining my stomach. *Welcome to the deep end of the eligibility pool—I hope you're a good swimmer.*

Four

INTAKE TESTING

As we all file out behind Eric, I look up at the large building in front of us. Building is really an understatement—it's more like a full complex. This particular building is wide, and curved like the large teardrop driveway we've parked in. The facade has evenly-spaced white columns across the full-length veranda and balcony.. If I didn't know better, I'd say we'd been transported back to an old-time southern mansion. This one is in perfect repair, not in plant-ravaged tatters like others we'd passed between here and Jackson Flats.

"Hey, where are they taking our stuff?!" Nell asks in a panicked voice. I spin and see that several uniformed men are taking our bags from Todd and heading off into a completely different building.

Eric cuts in, smooth as butter, "No need to concern yourself, darling. The staff are just taking them to your rooms, so your things will be waiting for you when you're done with today's testing. All of your personal items will remain unmolested in your new home. Just that way is the Future Mothers' Residence Hall, where you will all be staying while you're with us." I mentally cringe. Would it kill him to just call us women? "Now, come along, ladies—pool intake is just this way." He turns and walks off, clearly expecting us to trail after him. Which we do, so that's a point to Eric.

The interior of the building is just as polished and beautiful as the outside. It's surprising, actually, that this place is as shiny as the brochure promised. Frankly, I'd expected it to turn out more like one of those restaurants with pictures of the food in the menu, where what shows up never looks like the picture. After going down a few hallways, we are led into what looks like an upscale doctor's office. Pictures of pregnant women in white flowing gowns adorn the walls, as well as huge portraits of babies with chubby cheeks and gummy smiles.

Eric walks right up to the receptionist's desk, and hands over his tablet for inspection. She quickly taps a few times, then hands it back to him, never looking up or acknowledging us as we stand in the entryway. "Ladies! No need to stand around, please, make yourselves comfortable!" he gestures to the chairs spread around the room. They might be comfortable, if we hadn't just spent four of the last five hours sitting on a shuttle. Are they really taking us straight to have medical tests done, not to our rooms, or giving us a night to settle in first?

Almost before I finish my thought, a woman in pale pink scrubs and a clipboard arrives at a side door. "Margaret? If you'd please come with me."

Margaret stands with a flounce, and follows her. As she walks through the door she tosses a haughty look at us over her shoulder, as if she's won a prize by being called first.

However, almost as soon as the door shuts behind her another nurse in identical pink scrubs comes to the door with another clipboard, "Beth-Ann? It's your turn, dear." Beth-Ann heads over and disappears behind her nurse through the doors. Over the next fifteen minutes, all of the other girls are called back one by one, until it's just me and Charlotte left in the waiting room. Eric has drifted back over to the receptionist, who's clearly flirting with him.

Charlotte is fiddling with the hem of her shirt, looking uncomfortable.

"Hey Charlotte?" I say quietly.

She looks up, but doesn't say anything.

"I am sure you overheard earlier at the restaurant what Margaret was saying —you know, that to be beautiful, you have to be thin." I pause, and she gives me a barely perceptible nod before casting her eyes back down to her lap, "I hope you know that we don't all feel that way. For what it's worth, I think you're lovely just the way you are. You are curvy, and kind, and with those gorgeous green eyes, any man would be lucky to have you. Plus, on personality, you've got Margaret beat hands down." I grin.

"You're too sweet, Sadie. Thank you for saying so." She looks up at me politely, but I can't tell if she believes me. Just then, my name is called by yet another nurse in pink scrubs. I reach over and clasp her hand in mine. "It's going to be okay, we'll get through this together." Then I stand up, and walk through the door.

I follow the nurse down to a room at the end of the hallway. She asks me to put on a thin paper gown, and steps out of the room to give me some privacy. Thoughtful, given I'm not in the habit of stripping down in front of complete strangers. I shuck my boots, jeans, and tank. I'm not sure if I'm supposed to keep my underwear and bra on, but I feel safer with them on, so I leave them. The paper gown is flimsy, and a bit scratchy. The two tiny ties aren't doing much for my modesty, but it's better than just clutching it closed. I settle onto the little exam table, and am examining the maternity and baby photos hung in this room when there is a single brisk knock at the door, before it opens.

A tall, good-looking male doctor enters the room, "Hello there," there's a long pause, as he taps on his tablet, "Sadie. Nice to meet you. I'm Dr. Mitch. I'll be the one overseeing your care here at the New Life Center. Before I get started, do you have any complaints I need to be aware of, or any pre-existing health conditions?" He finally looks up at me.

"Well, it would have been nice if you'd taken a minute to make sure I was dressed before you came in, but otherwise, no." I feel a bit snappy, given he just barged in here without making sure I was ready, or clearly having paid any attention to who he was coming to "care" for.

"Uhh, yes, I'm sorry," he stammers, clearly surprised I've complained about *him*, rather than a medical concern.

"Thank you," I respond. At least he has some manners.

"I guess we'll just jump right in with my list then. Please lie back, I need to start your exam." He turns, sets the tablet down, and snaps on a pair of gloves.

After a round of seriously unpleasant medical intake tests, the pink-clad nurse escorts me to an exit, and informs me that I should head to the dormitory until dinner time. She doesn't stick around to chat, so I am left to my own devices to find the dormitory. *Really, super warm, these medical personnel,* I think with annoyance as I make my way across the lush green lawn towards the large house Eric pointed out earlier. A plaque beside the front door indicates I found the right place, but I still let myself in the front door cautiously. Peeking my head around, I spot a sitting area with both Elena and Leigh chatting with mugs in hand. Well, mostly Elena is doing the chatting.

Leigh is sunk deep into a cushy chair, but nods enthusiastically. I shut the door, and head over to them.

"Hey guys, can one of you point me towards my room?" I ask, interrupting their conversation about who the most handsome bachelor in the Bachelor Book is that they've seen so far.

Elena stops gushing over somebody named Quaid's bedroom eyes to answer, "Hey Sadie! If you go down the hall, up the stairs and to the left, we're all in the same hall. Your room is labeled with your name. The rooms are *super* nice and we don't have to share a bathroom or anything! Can you believe it? We've got this freaking mansion practically to ourselves!" She is clearly pleased with the amenities, so that's something.

I give her a small smile, "Thanks Elena, you're the best." And leave them to their gossip. It makes sense those two have gravitated to each other, since they're the youngest in our group. Three years may not seem like much of an age difference, but in this situation it definitely feels like it. I walk back through the entryway and into a hall. The largest curved double staircase I've ever seen rests in the middle of a large room, decked out in yet more maternity and baby portraits. At least the gowns in these are colorful,but, come on—I'd take a portrait of puppies or just about anything at this point for some variety.

Heading up and to the left, I find the hallway lined with our rooms. My room is a few doors down, right across from Jenna's. Her door is shut, but I hear what I assume is her shower running and loud thumping music. I listen a minute; it's not my usual taste, but it's catchy. I turn and open my door. Inside I'm greeted by mostly cream-colored walls, and more of the rich wood floors the designers clearly favor here. I've got a small entryway, which opens into a sitting area with a loveseat and coffee table, bracketed by two gold toile wingback chairs. I run my hand over one as I walk by. Pretty, but rather stiff.

Further in I find a bathroom filled with flat, modern surfaces. Everything is white, shiny stone, with a clawfoot tub and a large circular shower, with the biggest showerhead I've ever seen. I can't wait to get in there, and wash the road trip and medical exams from my skin. I can feel them on me, like a too-tight glove. Past the restroom and a privacy wall I find the bed covered in cream linens. Above an old fireplace is a large TV with a welcome message scrawled in gold text.

Welcome to the New Life Center! We hope your stay with us is comfortable as you embark on your journey to motherhood. If you need anything, please dial 00 on the keypad.

I continue to the far side of the bed, where there is a small, convenient closet. Just as promised I see my rolling duffel has been brought up for me. Beside the closet is a large curtain covering a sliding glass door, which leads to the balcony. As nice as that sounds, right now I'd rather have a screaming hot shower. I grab my duffel and unzip it and reach for my toiletry case, but stop at what I see resting on top. Two small envelopes, both addressed to me in different handwriting.

My hand shakes slightly as I open the first one. It's a letter from Peter.

Sadie,

I'm sorry I couldn't be with you today to see you off to the New Life Center. I know this is going to be a big transition, but if anybody can find the positive in this situation, I know it's you. I hope you find someone who is strong, but kind.

Always My Best,

Peter

I put the note down, touched that he not only thought of me but arranged a surprise from afar. Gavin must have snuck these in when he loaded my bag into the truck this morning.

I quickly open the second note, and snort out a laugh as I read it.

Sadie,

Give 'em hell.

See you soon,

Teddy

Teddy is my youngest brother, and the impulsive one in the family. I wonder what he means by "see you soon." He will be done with his police training soon, but by the time I'm allowed to leave, he'll be long since out and on a new assignment. He has one year left to decide if he's going to join the program, or opt out like Cade did. I set the letters on my mantle where I can see them, then grab my toiletry bag and head for that shower.

Two long shampoos later and dressed in a fresh pair of jeans and a black tank, my stomach is grumbling too loudly to ignore. I head out, and spot a key fob hanging by the door. I shove it in my pocket, and head downstairs to see if any of the other girls have figured out what we'll be doing for dinner.

Before I even clear the bottom step I hear Beth-Ann's voice coming from the sitting room, "Can you believe those tests this afternoon? They seriously had to do twelve things the minute we got off the stupid shuttle? It's just rude, is all I'm saying. Besides, where I'm from, the boys at least take a girl for a milkshake before thinking they're going to be sliding into home base."

That's one way to describe a pelvic exam, I guess. I shudder, trying to block out the unpleasant memory myself. I finally round the corner and spot her captive audience. Everyone but Margaret is here, but there are also two new faces I don't recognize.

Jenna is the first to greet me, "Sadie! What took you so long? We're starving!"

"Sorry, I got lost in that glorious shower. Did they tell us where to go for dinner?" I address the most important question.

She points over her shoulder to another TV hanging on the wall, with a gold-scripted message,

Please return to the Main Hall, where you will be seated for dinner promptly at 7 PM.

Well, at least they plan to keep feeding us. The two new women walk over to me. One sticks her hand out and says, "Hey, I'm Josephine, but everybody calls me Jo."

"Hey Jo, I'm Sadie. When did you two get here?" I look over to the woman with her.

"Faith and I got here just after your group did, we must have just missed you at the *lovely* intake center." She rolls her eyes, "We're the group from North Georada."

"Oh, wow! There's only two of you?" I observe.

"Technically, just me," Jo looks at Faith pointedly.

Faith speaks up, "I'm originally from New Texas, but I'm down from the Winnipeg New Life Center right now."

"That's so far! How in the world did you end up in Winnipeg from New Texas?" I've never heard of anyone moving that far away outside of an NAA job, which doesn't make sense for a woman our age. Although, on closer inspection Faith looks a bit older, or perhaps just tired.

"Oh, it's a really long story, I wouldn't want to bore you," she demurred. Now that she's said where she's from, I can pick up a faint hint of a drawl.

Nell butts in from across the room, "It's not like we've got anywhere better to be for another . . ." she checks the time on the announcement board, "ten minutes."

"Well, if you insist." Faith begins with resignation, "I entered the marriage program at eighteen in New Texas. I had one match, Bill. He was nice enough, and we were married within a few months. After just shy of two years, Bill was called home due to a death in the family. So, we actually got a home visit earlier than usual. We were given leave to go ahead and move back to his home to help with closing up his late aunt's house. She didn't have any heirs to leave it to other than him." She pauses reflectively and then continues, "A year later, we went back to the New Life Center to dissolve the marriage since we still had no children."

"Hold the phone," Leigh interjects, "You were married to the guy for three years and they just . . . ended it, just like that?"

Faith nods, "Yes, that's how it works. We were deemed 'incompatible' and put back into the pool to try again."

Leigh's mouth is agape. Elena takes over, "But, what about Bill? Do you miss him? Did you love him? Was he good in bed at least?" Beth-Ann laughs and then covers her mouth, and Leigh smacks Elena on the arm.

"Elena, you can't just go around asking people if their ex-husbands were good in bed! That is private information!" Leigh splutters.

With a chuckle, Faith gracefully answers, "Bill was a very nice man, but there were no fireworks between us. We parted as friends, and he chose to leave the program after our separation."

It's Nell's turn to ask, "Wait, but you said you were headed down from Winnipeg. How did you end up all the way up north when you were in New Texas?"

"Yes, I started in New Texas. But other than Bill, there were no matches in the tri-state above sixty-five percent. Bill had been a seventy percent match, so the medical team assumed I'd fail with a lower match, too."

"Well isn't that just peachy of them," Jenna mutters under her breath.

Faith shrugs, "Well, to be fair, they were probably right. So, I was put into the eligibility pool again, and the highest match they found for me was in Winnipeg. They sent me up to meet him, and we were married later that month."

Elena interrupts again, sounding nervous this time, "Wait, you only got one match again? And they made you move to Winnipeg for him?"

"Yes, he owned a ski outfitter shop in the tri-state, so his location was fixed."

"Is that what that means? I saw that in the Bachelor Book, but I didn't know what it meant. So they can just refuse to move?" I ask even though I'm pretty sure I know the answer.

"Yes, since the men have the ability to opt out, they're given more flexibility. If they have a legitimate reason to stay in their home tri-state, such as an ill relative or a local business, you'll have to go with them when the honeymoon is over."

Everyone is quiet for a heartbeat, as that sinks in.

Beth-Ann breaks the silence this time, "Well, how was your second match? Was he nice like Bill?"

"Well . . . I guess he could be when it suited him. But he was not pleased to be saddled with me, knowing I'd already failed the program once. Also, I think I was older than he expected when he signed up, but once you're matched, you have to see out the marriage term. Let's just say we were both happy to be separated once our time was up," she admits.

Elena looks troubled, "So even with two matches, you still haven't been able to get pregnant? I thought it was pretty much guaranteed with all of the testing and, I mean, isn't that the whole point of us being in this program?"

Jenna butts in angrily, "And what, you're just going to keep getting shuffled all over the NAA from man to man, until it works? IF it works? That's messed up, you should get to live your own life. How long has it been since you've seen your family?"

Faith casts her eyes downward, looking distraught, "I did get to go home last year." Her voice is quiet, subdued, "My father was killed in a work accident, and my husband let me go back to New Texas for the funeral." Gasps of sadness and disbelief sound from all over the room.

"God, Faith! I'm so sorry!" I say as I grab her hand, and squeeze it tightly. "He didn't even come down with you?" Surely you can't be *married* to someone and be that indifferent.

"No," she shakes her head, "It was the busy season for his business. He bought me a train ticket and I went on my own. It was probably for the best; my extended family wouldn't have liked him, regardless. That would have just added more stress."

For some reason that shakes me more than anything else she's said. I have spent my whole life admiring my parents, who had this soul-deep affection for each other. And here is Faith, being passed from man to man like a possession, and that man couldn't be bothered to attend her father's funeral with her? It sends a chill down my spine. This is unacceptable, and my heart hurts for her.

Nell is the one who speaks up next, sounding more calm than I think any of us feel right now, "Well, it sounds like it's a blessing that husband number two is in the past. I can't imagine you saddled with anyone that cold for the rest of your life." She lifts her chin, and looks Faith right in the eye, "Sometimes life dumps you in a pile of crap, but it doesn't mean you can't claw your way out of it." With that, she gets up and walks towards the entrance to the house. It takes me a minute, but I realize it's 7:05. We're late for dinner.

FIVE

THE RIOT ACT

I wake with a start, rubbing the blurriness from my eyes and looking around my bright room with confusion, wondering where the wind chime sound drifting through my room is coming from. My attention is drawn to the mini-tablet plugged in next to my bed. Yep, sure enough. There is an alarm, and a notification. I click on the icon, and an itinerary pops up. Breakfast is served in half an hour, and I've been assigned to a class schedule. What could they possibly be sending me to class for? Baby-making 101? How to be docile? Ugh.

Twenty-seven minutes later, I emerge from my room with my hair in a braid, and my signature jeans ensemble. I am not a morning person, so there better be some caffeine at this breakfast or somebody will be on the receiving end of a serious grouch-fest. I meet Faith in the hallway as she's leaving her room.

"Want to walk to breakfast with me?" I ask.

"Sure, thank you for offering," she responds with a small smile.

"Of course! We may as well enjoy each other's company while we can." I smile back.

"True, we won't have long, but at least we aren't alone. It's nice you came with such a large group," she says as we make our way down the stairs.

"Have your groups been small each time?" I ask, genuinely curious. It wasn't lost on me that the shuttle we arrived on only had ten seats.

"Yes, my first group was me and two others from my tri-state. In Winnipeg, there were five of us."

"So, have they told you who they are matching you with down here? I assume they've already got someone or they wouldn't have made you travel here, right?" At least I hope they wouldn't just move her around without a potential match.

"Right, but, I don't have any details yet. Well, there is one detail, which is kind of exciting." She hesitates.

"Really, what do you know?" I press.

"He's a ninety-nine percent match for me. It's the highest I've ever gotten. I might actually have a chance of this being my last husband." She looks petrified and excited in equal measure.

"Whoa! Those are really great odds. What were your other matches?"

"Bill was seventy percent, Spencer, my second husband was seventy-seven percent." She recalls matter-of-factly.

It's amazing to me how she can talk about all of this without more emotion. I don't think I could do it if I were in her shoes. My throat tightens. *Please God, don't let me end up in her shoes.* "That's really amazing, Faith. I'm sure this guy will be the one to give you a baby. And maybe he'll be really nice, too, like Bill."

She nods, "Well, he has to be better than Spencer. And at least if I have a baby this time, when our required time is up, I can go back to New Texas."

"Are you really homesick? Do you have more family there?" I hate to pry, but she's been so open, I hope she won't mind. We've made it to the main hall, but stopped just off the porch.

"I have an aunt and uncle, and one cousin. But, my parents' home is closed up and waiting for me, if ever I can get a release to go back. It sounds kind of heavenly to have a place all to myself, with no one telling me where I have to be, or who I have to live with. At first I so wanted to just settle down and live that perfect family life, but I don't know if that's even in the cards for me anymore. Two husbands in, and I just want to steer my own ship now, you know?"

I nod, it makes perfect sense to me. "I've only been dealing with all this for a day, and I don't want anything more than to run home and get back to my real life. None of this feels real to me yet." I look down at the grass and scuff it under my boot.

"It didn't become real for me the first time until I met Bill. Give it time, you'll find your feet." She gives me a brief side hug before starting up the porch steps.

I follow her, wishing I felt half as confident as she did that I would make it through this in one piece. We head into the dining hall for breakfast, get our plates and sit down with our group. Margaret, as usual, is sitting at the very end of the table, as far from us as possible. *Shocker.*

Around a mouthful of waffle, Nell asks, "Does anybody know what these classes are that we have for the rest of the day?"

"It's the rest of the week," Charlotte answers, "but I'm not sure what they're about."

"It's probably some boring, BS topic." Jenna says angrily. "God forbid they let us actually learn something useful, or a real job skill." She viciously stabs a piece of sausage with her fork.

"Jenna, they clearly don't care what's in our heads. Just our baby boxes," Josephine says, her acerbic humor like a dark cloud today.

"Hey, what did that sausage ever do to you?" I can't help but laugh at her as she sticks her tongue out at me in response.

Margaret sighs from the end of the table, "What are you, five? Have some dignity." She sneers at Jenna. "And they are teaching us what we need to know to perform our *current* duties. I spoke with Eric about it last evening at dinner, and he said we'll be learning about reproduction, fertility, and infant care basics." She spears a piece of fruit with delicate precision before continuing, "But if you ask me, they should add a class on basic table manners." That's interesting, as we hadn't seen her or Eric at the dining hall last night. I'd assumed she'd just stayed in her room.

"Oh, don't act like butter won't melt in your mouth." Beth-Ann interjects. "We're all in the same boat; this would go a lot better for us all if you'd act like a normal human on occasion." She's eating a piece of plain toast and has a cup of tea but doesn't seem to be enjoying either.

"All right, all right." I give Beth-Ann a pointed look before saying, "Thanks for telling us, Margaret." Beth-Ann drops it, but smacks my shin under the table with her foot. "Hey! I'm just trying to keep the peace." She smiles as if she has no idea what I'm talking about, and takes a sip of her tea.

"Faith, haven't you already taken these classes? Are they making you take them again? That seems like an epic waste of time," Jenna points out.

Faith nods, "I have taken them twice. Unfortunately, every time you get reassigned to the eligibility pool, they make you retake the classes."

Josephine rolls her eyes, "Don't they know the entire world is infertile? It's not your brain causing you not to get pregnant."

A few redundant classes aren't going to solve that.

Faith shrugs, "There's no point in arguing. If they want me in class, I have to be in class."

The chatting resumes as we all finish breakfast. As the last person is pushing her plate away, Eric strides into the room, wearing another suit. This one is electric blue, with a striped tie. "Ladies!" He booms from the doorway. "How is everyone feeling today? Excited to start your Future Mothers training course?"

There is a general murmur, but Margaret pipes up above the rest of us, "Of course, Eric, we're all just happy to be useful!" I swear that's the most chipper I've ever heard her.

He gives her a toothy smile, "Fantastic, that's what we like to hear! Is everyone's room to her liking?" We all nod in response, and he continues, "Perfect, that's what I like to hear! If you'll all follow me, I'll escort you to the auditorium for your class."

We all stand and he leads us out the back of the main hall to another building. On the way, he points out the entertainment hall, where the teaching auditorium is located, as well as a large gym, and another separate sports building. Right before we head into the building, he tosses out, "Oh, and I don't know if any of you are into equestrian sports, but if you follow the path to the left of the entertainment hall, it will lead you to the stables." He turns and holds the door for us, as if he didn't just make my day.

"There are horses here?" I blurt out, unable to contain my excitement.

Margaret rolls her eyes, "No, I think they keep unicorns in the stables. Good night, the company I am forced to keep here would drive a lesser woman to drink." She sashays past me into the building.

Eric laughs as if it's the funniest thing he's ever heard, "Yes, there are horses. If you would like to try riding lessons, I can arrange an instructor for you."

I'm almost shocked out of my boots to hear Leigh speak up, "Eric, Sadie here could teach your instructors a thing or two. Her family owns a ranch, she's been riding her whole life." She links her arm through mine, like she has Elena's on her other side. I just give her a smile, and we walk through the door together, ignoring Eric's look of surprise.

In no time, we're all seated in a mid-sized auditorium with spiral-bound books and pens in front of us. A pink-scrub-clad nurse with midnight-black hair enters, and starts a video for us. After an hour on the female reproductive cycle, she hands out a small pink wristband to each of us.

"These wristbands are to be worn at all times outside of the shower or bath. It tracks your temperature, heart rate, and several other key indicators which track your fertile cycle. After one to two months, it will be able to predict within a twenty-four-hour window that you are ovulating, and will notify you with an indicator on your wrist." She holds up a glowing wristband with a large pink heart flashing on it. These wristbands are key to helping you conceive quickly, so should be worn at all times." She reiterates, clearly not trusting us to follow her directions with just one warning. Faith shifts uncomfortably next to me, but keeps quiet.

Josephine raises her hand, and the nurse points to her. "If the genetic matches and these wristbands are so magical, why is the birth rate still dropping? Shouldn't things at least be holding steady by now?"

The nurse doesn't take offense, just sounds bored, "Unfortunately, the genetic damage done to humans as a whole makes conception very difficult. Scientists calculate that our population rates would be dropping over thirty percent faster if it wasn't for the program, and the technology we're able to utilize."

"Yeah, but is thirty percent really a big enough deal to make this mandatory for every single woman? Why can't we still have jobs, and just have kids later when *we're* ready?" she persists.

"That was actually the governmental direction until recently. Population size and birth rates have been closely tracked ever since the discovery of the Sterilization Vector, and in the last twenty years the world population has plummeted to lows not seen since the 1700s. If we're not able to stabilize those numbers soon, even tri-states won't be able to maintain sufficient populations. This was the agreed-upon solution to stave off further governmental restructuring and continued population declines," she reasons.

"It just doesn't seem right that the justices can all get together and make that kind of decision for us." It's Jenna who speaks this time. "Some of us want to live our own lives, not become baby factories. I want to get a paying job so I can support myself, not be reliant on some man I just met."

"Well, it's covered in the videos later this week, but I can mention it now—motherhood actually *is* a paid profession now. For every child born to a mother who's attended this program, she will receive a stipend for the rest of her life. In addition, there are bonus stipends if you and your husband opt to participate in one of the offered genetic diversity programs and successfully carry those children."

This time it's Charlotte whose hand goes up, and the nurse points to her, "What's a genetic diversity program?"

The nurse sighs, "This is all covered in your videos over the next week. The genetic diversity programs are available to any mother who successfully carries two babies to term with her husband. She will then be assigned a different sperm donor, and through in vitro fertilization have the possibility of carrying additional children from another father. This helps keep the gene pool wide, and ensures the health of the human population long term."

Charlotte's eyebrows climb so high, they are almost hidden behind her bangs, "Who are all the sperm donors? Like, another woman's husband, or . . .?" she trails off.

"No, in order for a man to opt out, he is required to provide sperm to the sperm bank to ensure his genes are preserved, as he may be the only viable match for a woman in the future. Now, if you will all allow me to start the next video, I'm sure it will answer some of your questions." She turns her back to us, and flicks on the next video without waiting for a response.

The video drones on about the matching process, and how every woman will receive at least one match. Historically, multiple matches are possible, but rare. The current record is four matches of seventy percent or higher.

I tune out the rest of the video as I think over the information she just dumped in our laps. Every time I think I've got somewhat of a handle on this whole situation, there is a new facet that comes to light. How many men are really okay with having their wives carry another man's baby? Even if it is done scientifically, in a lab? And raising another man's baby? Although she said it was optional, a big part of me wonders how true that is, given this whole program used to be optional, too. It feels like they keep finding ways to dig deeper into controlling our futures.

I feel panic creeping up my throat. I had been keeping myself grounded with the idea that this was all just for a season. Two years with a virtual stranger. Two years without a hug from my own family. Two years without getting a good morning snuffle from Morgan when I meet him at the pasture fence. It sounds like eternity, already. But I'm supposed to be able to get married, have a baby, go home with the baby and the husband,

and get back to normal. But now, the fact that they want to still be *managing* me two kids later makes my skin crawl. I surge to my feet, causing several of the other girls to turn in my direction. The nurse snaps a look at me, and I stammer out, "I need to go to the restroom."

I quickly go out the door and shut it behind me before she can argue. I lean my back against the door for a minute, trying to calm my racing thoughts, my pounding heart. It's going to be okay; it has to be. I can get through this. One day at a time, I can get through this. As I'm giving myself this mental pep-talk, I hear a man clear his throat to my left, and almost jump out of my skin.

"Good God, where did you come from?" I practically shout, as I turn and see him standing a few paces away.

He raises both hands in front of him, trying to assure me he isn't a threat, "Hey, whoa, let's calm down. I'm Patrick, I'm one of the guards here. I could tell you didn't see me, and didn't want you to be surprised, although I guess I missed the mark on that one." He offers a self-deprecating smile, and thankfully stays where he is.

I look down, and see that he is indeed wearing what appears to be a guard's uniform, although it's a little less obvious than guards you'd see at a bank, or with a justice when they visit town hall. "I didn't know there were guards here." I state, trying to get my brain over the shock and running again. I quickly take in his black hair, and the lean muscles under his uniform.

He smiles, "Well, they called in more of us last night, but we mostly stay out of your way in the guard shack near the entrance. It's very safe here; we try to keep it that way but still be unobtrusive. Are you out of class for a reason? Do you need something that I can help you with?" he offers politely.

"Uh, no. Just headed to the ladies' room." I start to walk away from him, towards the nearest restroom.

"Are you sure that's all?" he presses me, taking a step forward, "You seemed pretty upset when you came out. I really am here to help, with whatever you need."

"No, no, I'm fine." It's a small lie, but I have just met this man—he doesn't need to hear about my problems. Even if his eyes do make me want to confess it all. They are a deep, dark blue, and it feels like I'm compelled to lean into them for a closer look. *Pull it together, Sadie.* I mentally chastise myself. I smile politely at him and turn again for the bathroom.

I take a few moments to splash cool water on my face, and take a few deep breaths. I am stronger than this situation, and no matter what curve balls they throw at me, I am *not* going to buckle. I am a Taylor. If I could survive growing up in a small town with six big brothers, I can survive this. With that final thought, I straighten my braid in the mirror, turn on the heel of my boot, and shut the door firmly behind me. Chin up, Sadie. Give 'em hell.

As I approach the classroom door, I see Patrick standing a little way down the hall, alert but not uneasy. He really is a handsome man. If our matches are half as good looking, I don't think any of us would complain. He's got a really strong bone structure, and an honest face. Plus, you know, biceps the size of my head don't hurt, either. He raises a hand in a small wave, and I realize I've been caught checking him out. I quickly toss up a return wave and let myself back into the classroom, cheeks burning red. Thankfully the video is still playing, and the lights are dimmed so no one will notice

I can't help but wonder why they feel the need to guard us, but that's another problem for another day.

After the second day, the week takes on a monotonous pattern: wake up to windchimes, dress, eat with the girls, attend classes, lunch break, more classes, dinner, exercise regimen, fall into bed. I told everyone at dinner that night about the handsome guard, but we didn't see him or any others after that day, so clearly they didn't intend for us to know they were there. Jenna and Josephine are both convinced their sole purpose is to stop us from trying to run away, or else why would they hide them from us?

Faith then told us that a girl from her Winnipeg group had tried to run and didn't come back after her attempt, so they assumed she'd been successful at the time. Now, we had to suspect they'd just taken her somewhere else. Was there a New Life Center for girls who caused trouble? Who would want to take on a wife that was a known runaway? All these questions we discussed at length, but had no answers to. We probably would never know, as we'd made it to the last day of our training week now, and all we'd learned was a thorough accounting of human reproduction, including reproductive assistance technology and procedures we might need to help with conception, and all of the laws we were expected to abide by that regarded reproduction in the NAA, which was what they were recapping for us now.

"Ever since the Sterilization Vector was released, birth control has been illegal. As such, we take sex in all forms *very seriously*. There is no longer protection available to prevent STDs, STIs, or any other communicable disease, because those all prevent pregnancy as well. You are not to ever engage in a sexual relationship with anyone except your husband, and in order to join the program, he signed a binding agreement to be exclusive with you as well, for the term of the agreement. Nevertheless, you've all received screening as part of your intake testing, and will be screened throughout your time in this program at regular intervals," the nurse states, "A healthy, full-term pregnancy is our ultimate goal here, and these rules are in place to protect your future children. Society needs you to stay healthy, and this is how it must be done."

Jo snorts from her seat but is ignored by the nurse at this point; it's been a long week. I agree with her sentiment, though. It's not like any of us *agreed* to any of this. *Society needs you.* That's a pleasantly misleading way for them to put it.

"There are severe penalties for any person breaking these laws and intending to prevent a pregnancy or have an illicit affair, and I'd strongly encourage you not to find out what those entail. Trust me when I tell you, no man is worth that." She looks down briefly, and the first hint of emotion she's shown this whole week briefly flits across her face before she schools her features again.

Elena raises her hand, "Something's been bothering me. If scientists were able to create the Sterilization Vector to begin with, why can't our scientists now just switch it back? Create something new, as a treatment?"

The nurse frowns, but it seems like a reasonable question to me.

"Scientists in the past discovered that a gene therapy could be used to provide birth control, and essentially turn off your ability to reproduce. At the time, it was hailed as a leap forward for men and women who were done expanding their families. It started off small, and was touted for its safety and lack of side effects compared to other methods of birth control. What started out as a medical marvel, fell into the wrong hands."

That's the thing about humans, we can turn almost anything into a weapon.

"A group of environmental extremists got their hands on the therapy, and weaponized the delivery vector so that instead of only going to one patient, it would spread like the common cold. Then they put it into the water supply all over the globe. By the time doctors realized that more and more couples were turning up for fertility treatments with unexplained issues, the damage was already done. The majority of the world's population had been spreading the genetic virus, symptom free, for months."

She pauses the grim recounting of our history, and looks down for a moment.

"In the years since, birth rates have stayed significantly lower than they were before the genetic modification. Scientists' best efforts have allowed some births to happen, but now only two people who are near-perfect genetic complements have any chance of conception. As a result, gene therapy is now illegal, and it has been widely agreed that further tampering with reproductive genes could worsen the situation. "

She clears her throat, "Now, that is the last of the material we have to cover for you this week, so you have officially completed your future mother's training! Congratulations, and I hope the information serves you well." Someone mutters, "Thank God," but I can't place who it was before the nurse continues, "If you'll all head to the main dining hall, Eric and Dr. Mitch will be waiting with some news on the next phase of the process."

Great, my two favorite people. This week just keeps getting better.

SIX

SPREADING THE NEWS

T he ten of us file into the main dining hall, and our moods are pretty light since we're finally done with the least interesting training videos known to woman-kind. "I'm just saying, for videos about reproduction, they were the least sexy things I've ever seen," Jenna reiterates for at least the tenth time this week.

I groan, "Jenna, would you let it be? It's finally over. Let's all move on and pretend it never happened."

She, of course, doesn't let it drop. "Okay, but you can't tell me we wouldn't all be more interested if it wasn't made to sound so . . . *clinical.* It's bad enough we're almost all going into this as virgins. It's worse to think that the honeymoons we were promised are just going to be scheduled baby-making sessions. YAWN. Can't they at least let us have a little excitement in this whole process? No, just me?" She looks around for support, but none is forthcoming. "Y'all are no fun!" She finally lets it drop.

Eric has clearly caught the tail end of this conversation, as he stands and clears his throat uncomfortably. "Ladies! How are we this afternoon? Excited to be done with your training program?"

A few of the girls nod, but the rest of us just wait for him to tell us why we're here. Once he realizes that none of us are going to answer him, he breaks the news. "Well, tonight is the big night! I hope you've all packed a nice dress, because tonight is the night you meet your matches!" We collectively suck in our breaths at that, which only amps him up further, "That's right, at least one of you has more than one match to choose from."

Dear God, please let it be me. Please don't let them saddle me with just one terrible option. I feel selfish even thinking it, as no one in this group deserves to be saddled with a bad option. But I hope I have at least one choice, regardless. *Please be someone that will fit in with my family, please, please, please.* I glance around at the others, and see that we're all processing in different ways. The youngest girls look excited again, whereas Charlotte looks resigned, and Faith actually has a hopeful smile. I am sure I've got a look of dread, but I'm trying to school my face into something neutral, if not positive.

"You have two hours to prepare to meet your future husbands. If any of you do not have something suitable for the occasion, a few racks of dresses have been assembled upstairs in the wardrobe room, down the right hallway. Feel free to choose anything you'd like for the occasion. Everyone except Beth-Ann and Charlotte, you are dismissed."

Beth-Ann and Charlotte both freeze, looking at each other, and back to Eric, "Is everything all right?" Charlotte asks quietly.

"Yes, yes, I'm sure all is well. Dr. Mitch needs to speak with you each privately before you prepare for your evening." He gestures to the doctor, who's been standing silently this whole time.

"Beth-Ann, I'd like to speak with you first. If you don't mind coming to the conference room with me." Beth-Ann peels her fingers off of Charlotte's hand, which she'd been gripping tightly, before slowly following the doctor out of the dining hall.

Margaret is the first to leave, "Two hours? I'm supposed to meet my husband for the first time and you're only giving me *two hours* to get ready! This is ridiculous. I smell like a stale classroom—I'm not waiting around for the rest of you." She moves out the door the fastest I've ever seen her go. I shake my head at her retreating back. I'm in no hurry to meet my fate, so I'm going to wait with Charlotte.

The other girls start to trail after her, Jenna turns back when she realizes I'm not with them. "Sadie, you coming?"

"No, I'll wait for Charlotte and Beth-Ann. It won't take me two hours to get ready. You go on ahead."

"Suit yourself!" She turns and catches up with the rest of the group.

"Do you have any idea what they want to talk to you about?" I ask Charlotte.

"Not the faintest. God, I'm sure it's something bad. What if I can't have a baby? What if something is wrong with me? Can you get kicked out of this program for being defective?" She is starting to panic.

"Hey, it's going to be ok! Try to stay calm, we don't know what we don't know. I'm sure it's nothing major—maybe he just has a question about your family history or something. And I don't think any of us are getting off the hook, even if we do have issues trying to get pregnant. I mean, the whole world has issues now, right?" I try to reassure her, but she doesn't look any calmer.

We wait in tense silence for about ten minutes, just the two of us since Eric wandered off shortly after delivering his "great news." Finally, we hear two sets of footsteps in the hallway, and a pale Beth-Ann and Dr. Mitch come back into the dining hall.

"I'm ready for you now, Charlotte," Dr. Mitch says casually, looking down at his tablet again. She shoots me one last look of terror, before disappearing through the door with him.

Beth-Ann doesn't even make it over to me. She plops into the closest chair and puts her head in her hands. I quickly walk over and crouch next to her.

"What happened, Beth-Ann? Is everything okay? What did he say to you?" I rub the side of her arm, but she doesn't look up.

She starts to sniffle and leans against my shoulder. For a minute we just sit like that, her sniffling and leaning against me, before she finally manages to speak, "Well, he said there were some things in my health file that he needed to review with me, because some of my results were unexpected."

"Okay, is everything all right?" I encourage her to continue.

"Well, actually, yes. Turns out, I'm already pregnant," she says quietly. I'm shocked speechless for a moment, and she looks up at me with teary eyes. "It's Phil's. I guess we're a genetic match after all."

"Oh Beth-Ann, that's . . . I don't even know what to say! Are you happy? Are you in trouble? What's going to happen with you being matched tonight?" I'm not sure whether to laugh or cry with her, given the situation.

"Well, he asked me if I knew who the father was, and I said yes. He asked if the father was Phil, and since they already knew who he was, I said yes. I guess they have more information on us than we thought, since they knew about him. They said typically men aren't eligible to be matched so quickly after signing up but given the current situation they were going to make an exception and put my original match back into the pool. They didn't want word getting out that someone who was matched was already pregnant, so I don't know what they'll tell the guy, whoever he is."

I nod, since it sounds like that's the best possible option for Beth-Ann and Phil. "So, they're not going to penalize you, or cause you any trouble?" After the stern lecture we'd gotten from the nurse on illegal relationships, I don't know what to expect but I'm worried for her nonetheless.

"He said since Phil signed up for the program, they'll just let the match take place given we obviously were able to get pregnant, and that's the end goal. However, Phil technically has the chance to veto the match if he rejects that the baby could be his. I don't know what they'd do in that case, but Phil would never do that to me." She drags in a shaky breath, "But, they are going to bring up our marriage ceremony to tonight. And we don't get to go to a honeymoon destination, we'll be going straight to a pregnancy center for monitoring."

I give her a squeeze around the shoulders and lean back so I can see her better. "How do you feel about that? I know you and Phil wanted to be together, but that is a lot and it is fast."

She nods, "It is fast, but he's the one, Sadie. I'm sure of it. I'm mostly still in shock that I'm pregnant. Can you believe it? I have been feeling crappy, but I just assumed it was from the stress of leaving Phil and going through all of this."

I'd noticed her not eating much, but I had assumed the same thing she had. They tell us pregnancy is next to impossible, so nobody would jump to that conclusion in her situation. "So, you're getting married tonight, to Phil. I guess that means that double congratulations are in order!"

She finally smiles at that, but it dims after only a moment, "What if Phil's mad? He definitely didn't think any of this would happen so fast. I mean I know we're supposed to have kids but I assumed it would take a couple years to get there. What if he's not ready?"

"I don't think he would have signed up to try and match with you if he weren't ready for any possibility. He's such a genuine guy, I'm sure it's going to be okay. Just wait until you see him in a few hours, and I'm sure everything will click right back into place." At least I hope so, for her sake. I can't believe she's actually pregnant!

She looks lost in thought for a moment, but the sound of footsteps in the hallway breaks our bubble, signaling the return of Charlotte and Dr. Mitch.

"I wonder what they wanted from Charlotte. You don't think she's already pregnant, too, do you?" Beth-Ann asks me.

"No, somehow I doubt it. She didn't mention a boyfriend, or anyone from home actually." I respond.

Charlotte walks back in alone, looking shell-shocked and deflated, much like Beth-Ann. She woodenly walks over to us, and sits in the chair right next to Beth-Ann. Her chin wobbles as if she might cry, but she doesn't.

Beth-Ann reaches over and squeezes her hand before asking bluntly, "What's wrong? What did they tell you?"

Charlotte looks to her feet, "There's something wrong with me. They don't think I'll be able to get pregnant without having a procedure first, but they can't do the procedure at this center. They are sending me to the one in York to have it done by a specialist there."

"I'm so sorry Charlotte. Did they tell you what's wrong?" I take hold of her other hand.

"No, just that the specialist would explain when I get there, and it would take at least a week to recover. They are concerned that I got multiple matches, and they don't want to hold all of the men up while I'm in recovery. So they'd like me to let at least one of them go tonight, so as not to waste their time. The others will be traveling with me for the procedure and recovery."

Beth-Ann snorts angrily, "Waste their time? Must be nice to have the administrators worried about wasting their time, as if anyone gives two seconds of thought to *our* time and *our* inconvenience in this whole process! You have a legitimate medical concern, and all they care about is getting some guy back to work a week sooner, when this decision affects the rest of your life!"

"It really is ridiculous!" I agree, "Don't put pressure on yourself. Maybe there'll be an obvious dud, who you don't want to deal with for the next week. If so, you can send him packing. Otherwise, don't stress about it. If one of them can't support you through this, there's no way they'd be supportive through pregnancy and raising kids together," I rationalize.

"You're probably right, but how are they going to feel when they hear they've been matched with somebody who's defective, right out of the gate? What if none of them want to be matched with me at all!" Her chin starts to wobble again.

"Hey," I try to get her to look at me, "You are a beautiful person, inside and out. There is absolutely *nothing* defective about you. I hope you can believe that, but if not, you've got us to keep reminding you." I squeeze her hand, and she finally looks up.

"How do you do it, Sadie? How do you not let this get to you?" she looks troubled, and I don't have a good answer.

"I don't know, Charlotte. I guess there's not really any other option. I was raised to make the best of the situation, no matter what. When you live on a ranch, there are a million things that can go wrong any given day. A thousand possible emergencies, and you just have to deal, because by the time help gets there an animal could already be gone or injured beyond repair. So, I guess we just all know that you have to wade into the thick of it, and hope it works out on the other side. I have to believe that this is the same, that God and hard work will see me to the other side. Back to my family." I try to sound firm, and calm. If only I felt calm on the inside.

Beth-Ann speaks up, "Well, I guess we'd better go get cleaned up for our charming princes. Somehow, I don't think they'll be too impressed if we show up looking like raggedy messes."

I snort, "If they don't like me, they're welcome to see themselves out." But deep down, a small part of me is worried that they'll be disappointed in a plain farm girl from Georada. There's only one way to find out.

Roughly an hour later, we start to congregate down in the sitting area. I chose a simple green dress from home that pairs well with my light skin tone and a pair of silver sandals, but I see I'm one of the plainer dressed as each woman comes down the stairs. Elena chose a silver gown that sparkles everywhere the light hits it as she moves. Jenna's dress is extremely short and a bright electric purple. Beth-Ann's wearing what appears to be her prom dress, in a pastel yellow that hits just past her knees. Interestingly enough, we're all in completely different colors and styles—except for our identical tacky wristbands. It seems we had the same idea, to show our personalities with our clothing selection—everyone except Nell, that is, who looks extremely uncomfortable. She's in an expensive-looking black dress with a plunging neckline that she keeps tugging upward to no effect.

"Nell, I don't think that's helping anything." Josephine notes. "I think it's supposed to be low like that."

"I'm sure it is, but I don't want to flash any of these dudes the goods the first time we meet. This stupid thing is almost down to my belly button!" She sounds exasperated.

"Do you want to choose another dress? We don't have to be there for ten minutes." I suggest.

"It doesn't matter, I didn't bring any dresses and everything in that stupid room is just as revealing. I guess I'll just have to go like this." She is growing more upset by the second, and I can't stand it.

"I'll switch with you! You can wear my dress, and I'll go change into one from the room. If you want, I mean. You look beautiful, but you should be comfortable," I offer. Nell has been so steady, I can't stand to see her tortured more than she has to be.

She takes one look at my simpler dress, and lets out a huge sigh of relief, "Are you sure? I don't want you to be miserable, either. But yours looks a thousand times better than this monstrosity even if it will be a little short on me."

"I'm sure. Head to the room with me and I'll give you this dress." We both hurry up the stairs, and into the wardrobe room. I hadn't even gone in here originally, since I already had my green dress to wear. Hopefully I can find something that fits quickly. Beth-Ann and Faith followed us up here, and quickly help us change. I strip off my dress and hand it to Faith, and she turns to Nell who starts unzipping the black dress. Beth-Ann and I both head to different racks, hoping to find something quickly. The first rack is all black, strappy, revealing numbers that I wouldn't be caught dead in.

I turn to the next one, right as Beth-Ann shouts, "I think I found one! It's even green like your first dress!" I look around the end of the rack and I do like the color, but all resemblance ends there between the two dresses. This dress has a green lace top over a flesh-toned backing fabric, which slowly coalesces into a solid green skirt which drapes to the floor.

"Are you sure? That's going to look like I'm practically naked at the top. Oh, hell. How high does that slit go?" But she's already pulling it off the hanger, and shoving it towards my head.

"I'm sure, it's either put this on or go naked. We have two minutes before our escort arrives," she reminds me as she pulls the gown in place over my head.

Thankfully, it does cover all the most important bits, and you can't see through the nude backing. But as I look down, I'm sure it doesn't look that way to an observer. The green lace is sparse on my arms and chest and doesn't start to cover much until my ribcage. It is a really pretty lace pattern, at least. She hastily zips me, and we follow Nell and Faith back out of the wardrobe and hurry down the stairs. Margaret is just coming down the last few steps ahead of us, and she must have brought a custom gown from home. It's a shiny gold floor length evening gown, and fits her like a second skin before expanding into a mermaid skirt at the bottom. We make it to the entryway right as Eric lets himself in to escort us to the entertainment hall.

He lets out a low whistle as he rakes his gaze over us, "Ladies, you are about to make ten men very, very happy." His heavy glance lingers on Margaret for a heated moment, and he offers her his elbow. "If you'll follow me, it's time to meet your matches." He turns and walks back out into the twilight with Margaret by his side, and one by one we follow him to meet our fates.

SEVEN
GENTLEMAN CALLERS

W e file into the entertainment hall behind Eric and Margaret, and before we reach the banquet hall the sound of stringed instruments and male voices spills out to greet us. My stomach is clenched so tightly, I know there is no way I'll be able to eat a thing. I say one last prayer for calm as Eric opens the door, and then stands to the side for us to enter. I'm last in line, but I can hear the hush spread as the first few girls make their way into the room.

My first impression when I clear the doorway is that there are more men here than there should be. I know Charlotte had several matches, but even so I wasn't expecting a crowd quite this large. There have to be nearly twenty men here, which I wasn't expecting. I stop next to Beth-Ann, and scan the group. They are all staring back at us, just as we are at them. However, where you can practically feel our anxiety, they seem predominantly anticipatory. I guess it makes sense, since they are volunteers. I reach up and shove a piece of hair behind my ear that escaped from my braided crown, and realize that I recognize a face or two from the Bachelor Book.

If I'm not mistaken that is Devonte with the kind eyes towards the back of the group, and, oh my gosh— "Patrick?" I whisper, as I spot the guard standing next to him. Is he in the match program, or just here guarding this event? Beth-Ann elbows me, and I realize a few men closest to the front are staring at me curiously, having clearly heard me. I can feel my face burning, and quickly drop my gaze to the floor without scanning the remainder of the group. Thankfully, Eric chooses that moment to walk in front of us and start the evening.

"Welcome, welcome, everyone!" he says with his signature booming excitement, "We're so glad to have you all here today! I won't keep you waiting any longer to meet your perfect matches, so I will get straight to introducing each of these lovely ladies. If you are one of her matches, please come forward and I'll tell you which table you'll be seated at this evening."

He pulls out his tablet, and checks the table numbers, and then looks to his left where Margaret is standing with a serene smile. "First up we have the lovely Margaret." A suited man steps forward from the front of the pack. His tie is an icy silver, and his hair is swept back from his face and gelled to precision. He walks directly to Margaret and she offers her hand daintily.

"I'm Calvin Swift, and I'm absolutely enchanted to meet you, Margaret my dear." He leans forward slightly as if to bow, and then takes her hand and tucks it into his elbow possessively. Her expression never changes as Eric gives them a table number, and she's led away. No other men step forward, so I guess she only got one match.

Eric continues down the line and Elena is matched with a handsome, tan man named Hector. She blushes prettily when he reaches out and offers his hand. I am holding my breath when he introduces Charlotte and three men separate from the group and introduce themselves. My heart soars when I see that Devonte is actually here for her. Maybe all of these matches won't be so terrible, after all. After a moment of indecision, the three of them escort a furiously blushing Charlotte away towards the tables.

Jenna is matched with a man named Marcus, who's wearing a uniform rather than a suit. Leigh gets two matches; an older-looking man who introduces himself as Randy, and I see Faith stiffen as the second introduces himself as Spencer. *Surely* that isn't the same Spencer who is her colder than ice ex-husband? What are the odds? But the look on her face says that it must be. She looks horrified and mortified in equal measure. He, on the other hand, is soundly ignoring her and practically drooling over Leigh in her tight blue one-shoulder gown. Instead of taking her hand as all the previous men did, he slithers an arm around her waist, and I think I hate him even more in that moment. Leigh looks apologetically over at Randy, who follows politely as Spencer practically drags her out of line.

Next up is Josephine, who's standing with her chin held high and staring down the dwindling group of men. As Eric introduces her, a short, thin man with receding hair steps forward and introduces himself as Elijah. She looks him up and down once, and ignores his proffered arm before walking herself away to find a table. He trails after her, looking embarrassed. That is definitely not a match made in heaven.

It's Faith's turn, and I finally get up the courage to sweep my gaze over to the crowd of remaining men, and realize that everyone left must have several matches. There are far too many here for there to be any single matches left. My gaze stops, my heart drops out of my chest, and it feels like it bounces off every single bone in my body before crashing flat to the floor. I dimly hear Faith's name announced past the ringing in my ears, as my brother Teddy steps from the group. He shoots me a cocky grin before he saunters over to Faith and sticks out his hand for her to shake and introduces himself,

"Theodore Taylor, but everyone calls me Teddy. Nice to meet you, Faith."

Oh, God. Faith's ninety-nine percent match. *The match who she plans to pop out a baby with and then leave behind to return to New Texas* is my youngest brother, Teddy. I thought he was taking a year to settle into his career before deciding if he wants a wife. So why is he here, batting his long eyelashes at a shyly smiling Faith, instead of finishing up his training? I watch in shocked silence as he looks over his shoulder at me and mouths, "We'll talk later" as they walk off together towards a table.

I'm still in shock as I watch the largest man in the dwindling group walk forward to claim Nell's much smaller hand. He is built like a solid wall of muscle, and his stoic expression never wavers as he greets her and then leads her away. Nell casts a worried glance over her shoulder at Beth-Ann and me, the only two left to be matched. But they told Beth-Ann she'd be matched and directly married to Phil tonight, and her other match was sent home. I briefly glance at the remaining bachelors, but there are far too many men left. There is Phil on the right, with a wide grin aimed directly at Beth-Ann. As soon as Eric introduces her, Phil strides forward, grabs her around the waist, and plants the biggest kiss I've ever seen right on her lips. She reaches up and tangles her hands into his short brown locks, pulling him closer.

Eric looks scandalized, and there is a murmur from the bachelors. But they don't seem to care who's watching. In this world of crazy matchmaking, they got each other. And I'd be a liar to say my throat didn't tighten with both happiness and a tinge of jealousy for what they have.

Eric clears his throat loudly, "Excuse me, if you two would head on over to . . ." he looks down again, "table nine, we need to continue with the introductions."

They kiss for one last moment, before separating just enough for Phil to rest his hand on Beth-Ann's cheek carefully, as if she's made of porcelain. Then he twines his fingers through hers, and they make their way off to table nine. It's at that moment that I click back into reality and realize I'm alone up here with Eric. All eyes in the room are on me, and the gaggle of remaining dudes. Surely some of these guys were matched with someone else, because I vaguely remember one of the videos stating that the maximum number of matches received to date in the program was four. And there are more than four left. So, somebody got confused and missed his match.

Eric is back to business, though, and before I can open my mouth and say something stupid, he introduces me, "Ok! Last, but most certainly not least, we have the charming Sadie. If you are her potential match, please step forward!" He smiles widely, as if he hasn't said the same thing nine other times, and I barely keep my mouth closed in my shock as every remaining man steps forward at once.

A few of them shoot each other annoyed glances as they vie for who will greet me first. A man in a suit wins out, his hair trim and neat, and his teeth are as blindingly white as Eric's. He extends a well-manicured hand to capture mine, which he brings to his lips abruptly. "Hello, Sadie. I'm James. It's a pleasure to meet you this evening. I look forward to getting to know you more intimately in the coming days."

Okay, eww. I literally just met you. But I can't say that out loud, so I swallow my revulsion and try to be polite like my mama taught me, "It's nice to meet you as well. I'm sure we'll find time to chat." I give him a small nod as I firmly remove my fingers from his grasp. He doesn't look pleased with my tepid response, but I don't have time to dwell on it as another man steps forward.

This man is slightly more reserved, but I immediately like him better as he extends his hand to shake mine like an equal. "Hello Sadie, I'm Asher. I'm a veterinarian from the Saskerta Territories. I hope we'll get a chance to speak this evening."

"It's nice to meet you, Asher. I would like that as well." I give him a polite smile, and he returns it, crinkling the corners of his deep brown eyes. He seems genuine, and the polar opposite of James. Saskerta Territories are so far away, though, at least two thousand miles. That means one of us would have to move away from everyone we know if we marry. I try not to frown as he moves to the side and another man greets me.

"Hey, Sadie, I'm Pierce." This man is all smooth warmth as he reaches for my hand. He doesn't shake it, just holds it between us for a moment. I look from our joined hands up to his face. He's lightly tanned, with wavy blonde hair and piercing green eyes.

"Hello, Pierce." I'm not sure what to say, and we just gaze at each other for a moment. A girl could get lost in this man's eyes far too easily. He gives my fingers a squeeze and slips away from me to let the next man come forward.

"Sadie, nice to meet you. I'm Matthew Leeds from York." He's brisk, forthright, and he's got a tight grip as he gives my hand an aggressive shake.

"Hello Matthew, it's nice to meet you, too." I give him a firm grip in return, and he smiles.

"My friends call me Matt—you should, too."

"Okay, Matt, I hope we can become friends in time." He gives my hand one last pump up and down before releasing me, and straightening the sleeves of his gray blazer. On his left, the next man approaches. His outfit is one I'm intimately familiar with.

Decked out in a black cowboy hat, button-up plaid shirt, bolo tie, and clean denim, with boots, he is the definition of a cowboy. "Sadie, I'm honored to meet you this evening." He starts off with an easy smile. "My name is Grant, and I'm a rancher from Central Georada. I do hope to have the pleasure of your company for many evenings to come." He tips his hat in lieu of a handshake, and I give him a nod in return.

"Wow, nice to meet you Grant. My family runs cattle down in Jackson Flats. I'd love to talk about your operation sometime."

He looks pleasantly surprised, and his eyes flit down my floor-length green gown. "Well I'll be damned. I'd love that." He meets my eyes again and slowly tips his hat before he makes room for yet another man. How many are there at this point?

This man is suave, and I can tell he has no problem with the ladies. He's buff, and with his dark hair and friendly demeanor, I know he'll keep me on my toes. "Darlin', nice to meet you. I'm Antonio." He shocks me by going in straight for a hug. My cheek presses up against his silky patterned shirt, and I notice the top two buttons are undone. This close up, his cologne is nice, but far too strong.

"Oh! Uhm, hello, Antonio, I'm Sadie. It's a pleasure to meet you." I awkwardly pat him on the back a few times before he releases me.

He gives me an openly flirtatious look, not bothered in the least by the competition, "The pleasure is all mine, I promise you!" His eyes rake me slowly from my toes back up to my face, and I can feel myself turning red from his blatant perusal. I get that the end goal of this program is to start a family with one of these men, but I didn't think they'd be coming on so strongly to a woman they don't know from Eve.

I'm just starting to feel trapped under his heated gaze when a strong hand grips his shoulder, causing him to look accusingly at the next man in line before stepping aside. My brain catches up and follows the hand to its owner, and I suck in a breath. "Patrick?"

He gives me a warm smile, "In the flesh, Sadie. How are you holding up?" His other hand is in his pocket, giving him a casual but confident look.

I note he's still in his guard's uniform. "I'm okay, I suppose. Are you still working, or are we matched, or, uhm . . ." I trail off, not wanting to offend him, but not sure what to make of his presence.

"Turns out, we're a match. Ninety-nine percent, or so they told me. Can I show you to our table?" He extends his hand towards me in a friendly gesture. I grab it, and his palm feels warm and solid against mine. He entwines our fingers, and I walk in a cloud of suitors towards table ten. We arrive at a round table with eight seats, and a ubiquitous cream table cloth. A quick glance towards the rest of the room shows me that each table is placed with the exact number of matches for the woman assigned to it.

Patrick pauses and pulls out the chair in front of a little vellum card with my name on it in elegant script. I sweep my skirt to the side so I can sit, accidentally widening the thigh-high slit up the side as I do. "Oh, geez!" I quickly drop into the chair, and awkwardly try to wrestle the fabric back over my bare leg.

"Hey," Patrick stops me with a calm hand, and looks directly into my eyes, "It's okay. Nobody is going to see that under the table." Then he carefully tucks my chair in.

I know my cheeks must be red as the clay that's usually caked to my cowboy boots, but I force myself to look at him again, "Thank you, you're right." He's seated to my left, and Asher is to my right. Everyone else has settled around the table, and they seem to have witnessed my embarrassment over showing so much skin to virtual strangers.

Before I can drown in my own awkwardness, Asher smoothly draws my attention, "So, Sadie, would you mind telling us a little bit about yourself? For instance, where did you grow up, and do you have any siblings?" He reaches for the water pitcher in the center of the table, and starts filling up a glass.

"Yes, I'd love to." I grasp onto the topic of home and family like a rat clutching a floating board off of a sinking ship, "Well, I'm from Jackson Flats, towards the middle-eastern edge of Georada. I have six brothers, one sister-in-law, and two nephews."

"Did you just say *six* brothers?" Pierce interjects, looking shocked.

I nod, "Yes, I know it's odd now-a-days. But there are seven of us. I'm the youngest. Actually, Teddy, my youngest brother is right over—" I search for him and Faith, and spot them a few tables over, talking animatedly over a bread basket, "there!" I point to the table. They are so engrossed in their conversation that neither looks up. I wonder what they're discussing so intently?

"What are the odds? That's great that there's a familiar face here with you," Asher says as he hands me the cool glass of water.

I smile at him gratefully, "Thank you," and take a sip. As I look around the table, James has an almost predatory look in his eyes which gives me the creeps. I quickly skip past him and land on Matthew, who's also looking at me, but with calculation instead.

"What are the odds . . ." he repeats thoughtfully. "How often does a woman get matched with," he glances around the table, "seven bachelors at once? Aren't matches usually a little more one-on-one?"

Grant answers in a slow drawl, "Sadie here is clearly an exceptional woman, to have been a strong genetic match to all of us."

Matthew's eyebrows lower as he addresses Grant, "How strong of a match did they give you? I was told she wouldn't be matched with anyone under a ninety percent ranking."

Grant nods, "Ninety-nine percent."

Antonio pipes up, "Same, ninety-nine percent"

One by one, each man around the table agrees.

Holy fudge. There's no way I can be a ninety-nine percent match to all of them, is there? There *has* to be a mistake. How in the world am I supposed to choose if they're all the same ranking? I've got to change the subject. Patrick offers me the bread basket from the center of the table, and I choose the fluffiest roll I can see.

"So, can you all tell me a bit more about yourselves?" I ask before taking a large bite out of my roll. Mama forgive me, but I need to put something in my mouth besides my foot this evening.

They go around the table and each tells me their job, where they're from, and if they have any siblings or living family. I would kill for a notepad right about now. I'm desperately trying to remember all the facts they're telling me, when Patrick leans in close to my ear and whispers, "Relax, this is all in the Bachelor Book— you can catch up on the details later." Thank God. Politician, Actor, Businessman, Pro Soccer Team owner . . . I need a chart. Or, I don't know, a tape recorder.

Food is brought to the table by well-dressed waiters, and we all tuck in with different levels of gusto. Just as I'm going in for a second mouthful of my pasta, an odd staticky sound comes from my left, and I hear a voice that's not Patrick's.

"There has been a breach! I repeat, code four-one-oh, breach in progress. Return dolls to the dollhouse for lock-down protocol immediately."

EIGHT

THE DOLLHOUSE

T he voice stops, and before I have time to process what I just heard, Patrick grabs my hand and hauls me to my feet as uniformed guards start pouring into the dining room. People around the room are all scrambling to jump to their feet, but he doesn't wait as he starts pulling me to a side door, out of the fray. The rush of noise and people running dims slightly as the door shuts behind us. We're in a side hallway that I've never been in before.

Patrick hasn't let go of my hand, "Come on Sadie, hurry!" he urges me.

I use my free hand to grab at the heavy bottom of my skirt and haul it upwards to try to keep moving faster, "Patrick, where are we going? I didn't think there was anything back this way except the stables?" *Stables I haven't even had a free moment to visit yet* I think wryly. *Not the time, Sadie, not the time.*

We reach the end of the hall just as I hear a door slamming shut behind us, we both spin to see who's come through the door, and I sigh in relief to see that it's Teddy hauling a confused Faith behind him, straight towards us. "I hope you know where you're going, man. Everyone else was running the opposite direction!" Teddy whisper-shouts to Patrick.

"I do! Follow me, stay low, and try to be as quiet as possible just in case." He pulls open the door to the outside, and cautiously looks left and right before stepping out and waving for us to follow. Teddy and Faith catch up to us and follow hot on my heels. We tumble out into the dark night, and I'm surprised to see that this side of the building is completely unlit. Other than trimmed grass where we're standing, I see that we are a few hundred feet away from a stone-lined walking path. Beyond that is all forest as far as the eye can see.

Patrick raises his wrist to his mouth, and speaks quietly into what appears to be a smart watch, "Glitch, you copy?"

It's silent for a beat before I hear a man's voice quietly sprout from his watch, "What's up Rick-raff? You out in this madness?"

"Yes, and I could use some eyes on the security cams for safe routing. I'm escorting two dolls and a boy toy." Patrick is searching the ground for something, but I can't tell what.

Dolls? Boy toy? What in the ever-loving heck is he saying?

"I've got your back, where are you and where are you headed?" the voice responds immediately.

"I'm behind the EH, facing the west wood quadrant. We were instructed to return to the dollhouse if the path is clear," he responds in a low voice. He bends down, and pulls a large metal pole that had been hidden against the side of the building. He spins and quickly shoves it through the door handle, and it clears both sides of the door frame.

"Negative, route is not clear to the dollhouse. I've got three free agents in my line of sight. May I propose a backup location?" He asks before continuing.

"Shoot fast, Glitch. We're in the shadows but not secure here." Patrick confirms, reaching for my hand again. He looks down at my heavy gown, and sighs. "What kind of shoes are you wearing under that thing?"

"I'm wearing sandals, nothing crazy." I respond, and lift my hem so he can see the sparkly silver, but mercifully flat, shoe.

He nods, "What about you?" he turns to Faith. She wordlessly raises her hem enough for us to see that she is strapped into deep crimson heels that match her A-line gown. "Take them off quickly, and hand them to Teddy."

Faith squats down to remove the shoes as Glitch's voice comes back, snapping through the quiet of the barn, "Rick-Raff, I see two clear routes. One to the stable and then from there on to home base. I'll keep eyes on the security footage and notify you of any changes."

"Copy that, thanks Glitch." He's all business. "Ok ladies, hold your skirts, stay low, and don't stop running until we're inside the barn, understand? No matter what, you hit the side door running and don't stop, clear?"

I can feel the blood drain from my face, but I nod and crouch into a low stance. He gestures something to Teddy over my shoulder, and then he takes off in what I can only assume is the direction of the barn. I follow, and over the blood rushing in my ears I can hear two sets of feet running behind me. What feels like an eternity but was probably only two minutes later, I see a large, gorgeous barn come into view. It is white-painted wide wooden planks with a green metal roof, and surrounded by flood lights and well-manicured shrubs.

Patrick wordlessly points to the right side of the building, where I see a single door. We run straight to it, and he holds it open as I run through. I stop, and put my hands on my knees to catch my breath as a beat later Faith is hauled through the door with Teddy's arm around her waist. Patrick quickly slips in and yanks the door shut with a small snap. We all pause and listen for a tense moment, but I don't hear anything except the soft sounds of horses in a night barn and our labored breaths.

Patrick motions for us to stay where we are, and silently walks off down the barn aisle, peering into stalls and checking to see if we're alone. A minute later he returns, "We're fine for the time being, I want to clear it with Glitch before we try to make another run for it. Catch your breaths, because it's about twice the distance." He raises his wrist to his face, "Glitch, you copy?"

It's only a heartbeat before his watch speaks back, "Copy, Rick-Raff. Nice night for a jog?"

Ha-ha dude, ha-freaking-ha. Thankfully my breathing is already going back to normal. Poor Faith is still heaving against Teddy's side. My eyes narrow in his direction.

Patrick is all business and ignores the jab. "We're going to take a beat before making the run to home base. Keep an eye on the cameras and I'll give you a thirty-second warning before we go."

"Teddy, of all the places you could be, why on GOD'S GREEN EARTH ARE YOU HERE?" I am whisper-shouting at him by the end, trying not to startle the horses.

He startles slightly, eyes wide as he answers, "Did you really think we were going to let you come here alone? We all did rock, paper, scissors, and I lost on round four, so here I am." He tries to make light of the situation, "Well, I mean, not Phil because Tess would castrate him if he even looked at another woman."

I mean, it's sweet of them to try to protect me and all, but signing up for this mess seems like going overboard. If I hadn't been glaring at him so hard, I might not have noticed Faith deflate slightly in his grip. I dart my eyes pointedly at her, and back to him twice before he realizes what he just said. No woman should feel like a consolation prize, regardless of the circumstances.

"I'm not sure if that's sweet or just stupid, big brother. But I am glad to see your stupid face regardless." I lean over to hug him, and he lets go of Faith to return the gesture. Quietly I whisper, "Ix-nay on the osing-lay!" *You dummy*, I add in my head. He looks confused as he pulls back until I kick him in the shin.

"Ow, what the heck, Sad-ist!" He complains, but I give one last pointed glance to Faith and I see it dawn on him. He blushes slightly, "Oh, uh, Faith, I hope you don't take it personally—I hadn't even met you yet and you're lovely, I just didn't plan on getting married quite so soon, is all."

She gives him a small grimace, "No, not personal at all. If I didn't have to, I wouldn't be getting married so soon either." Her voice shakes slightly, but she tries to hide it.

My big, confident, bone-headed brother is stammering like a pre-teen. I would love it if it weren't for the fact that we were currently hiding out in the fanciest barn I've ever seen, hoping unknown people weren't here to do God-knows-what with us if they find us. I turn and look at Patrick, who's standing at alert off to the side, watching our interaction. He's got a miniscule grin but is trying to look unaffected. He quickly looks away as I make eye contact.

"Faith, have you got your breathing back to normal so we can go again? It's about twice as far this time, but there's more tree coverage so we can take it a hair slower." He sounds completely calm, as if this is nothing out of the ordinary.

She nods, "Yes, I'm ready," she says with forced confidence.

Patrick raises his arm and signals Glitch, "Thirty seconds to go time, hold the door for us."

"Heard; you're still clear," is all he says in return. Patrick spins and grabs hold of the door, and we all silently await his signal. A few seconds later he eases himself just far enough past the door to visually sweep the grounds, and then he takes off into the night. I follow right after him, and we bolt out into the well-lit grounds and towards the edge of the woods. When we are inside the tree line, he slows just enough for Faith and Teddy to catch us before following the edge of the woods around the clearing. It's dark here, so we are all jogging as quickly as we can without tripping and breaking something.

After what feels like an hour, the tree line curves sharply, and a squat building comes into view ahead of us. We are probably only a minute out at our current pace when I hear a hushed sound from Patrick's watch.

"Four-one-oh, 3 o'clock." Glitch states. Patrick halts instantly and throws a fist up over his right shoulder. He crouches down, and we all mimic the position. His eyes are locked on a spot just past the corner of the building, and he's pulling something from his boot.

"You keep a pistol in your shoe?" I ask, surprised by the sudden appearance of the weapon.

He shoots me a sharp look to keep quiet, and slowly advances to the edge of the open field. Right when I start to wonder what he's doing, I spot a black-clad figure walking past the corner of the building we'd been about to run to. He's wearing a mask, but by his build it's definitely a man. His gaze sweeps over where we're hiding without stopping, and he continues around the building towards the side door closest to us.

He lifts his arm as if to speak to the inside of his wrist, presumably into a device similar to Patrick's. At that second, I hear a large thud behind me, as if someone's fallen hard to the ground.

I spin to look and make sure Teddy and Faith are both okay, as the masked man shouts into his com, "Possible package sighting, North qua—" his voice cuts off as Patrick's pistol lets out a single, loud crack beside me. I turn back around and fling my hand over my left ear to try to stifle the ringing from the gunshot.

Before I can process the black figure crumpled on the ground, Patrick is yelling. "Move! Move! Move! Straight to the door! Glitch, we're inbound!"

My instinct is to check on Teddy and Faith again to see what made that sound, but Patrick doesn't give me the opportunity— he grabs my wrist and runs like the devil himself is after us. We approach the door, and it swings open seemingly on its own, and we don't slow down until we're past it and well inside a tan hallway. A thin, uniformed man is at the doorway. I turn as soon as Patrick drops my wrist and I am so grateful to see Teddy with Faith in tow, right behind us. The door slams shut, and the thin man slides a lock into place.

"Well, you sure know how to make an entrance," he quips lightly, as if there isn't possibly a dead body outside that door.

"Can you call for clean up, and I'll get the girls settled into a spare room?" Patrick is still all business, but this time reaches out and offers his hand for me to take. I can see hesitation in his eyes, but I don't feel any myself as I grab his hand and follow him down the ugly hallway.

A few minutes later, the men have deposited us into a room with bunk beds on one wall, and a bathroom. We immediately raided the closet and found some standard looking guard uniforms, which we quickly changed into from our torn up gowns. The patch on my chest says Guff, and Faith's says Sweet.

"I just feel so awful," she tells me for the third time. "If I wasn't such a klutz that man might have just moved on and still be alive." She is sitting on the edge of the bottom bunk, with her head in her hands.

"Faith, I know you feel responsible, but we didn't ask him to come here and try to start all this. We could have been kidnapped, or worse. I'm not saying it's okay that he's dead, but I am saying it's better him than you." I'm across from her in a desk chair. I rake my fingers through my messy hair and find a leaf. I pick it out and toss it into the small round trash can beside me.

She looks up at me with tears in her eyes, "Is it, though? Nobody wants me, Sadie. I can't have a baby, so I'm useless. Nobody cares about me, and nobody would have missed me if I was the one laying out there on the ground. Even your brother, sweet as he is to you, is only here for *you*. He doesn't want anything to do with me, or to have a baby with me." She sinks her head back into her hands and begins to sob.

"Hey," I cross the room to sit next to her on the bunk, "Hey, that is *not* true." I put my arm around her shoulders and lean into her side, "I would miss you. And you know what? If my brother had to be married to somebody in our group, I'm glad it's you. You are the most genuine, kind person I've met here. And no matter what's been thrown at you in your life, you made it out on the other side. That says something about what you're made of. You are a fighter, whether you believe it or not." I give her a squeeze, as if I can force my words to take root with her.

"It doesn't feel like it. It feels like I've just been broken down into a puppet, and tossed around from man to man until someone eventually gets what they want from me. How is that fighting, Sadie? I'm only still standing because I do what I'm told." She's still sniffling, but the body-shaking sobs have stopped, at least.

"You are a fighter. Sometimes living to fight another day is the only option available to us, and you have done that. You are in the ring for round three, and you are still smiling. You are not broken, and you are not worthless. We are going to be sisters soon, and I don't let anybody talk about my family like that, understand?"

She looks up again, and lifts one side of her mouth wryly, "I've never had a sister before—I'm not sure I'll be any good at it."

I smile at her, "Don't worry, I'll teach you."

There is a soft knock on the door, and I recognize it's Teddy from the shave-and-a-haircut pattern. "One second, Teddy." I cross the room and unlock the door.

Teddy is on the other side, with sandwiches and water bottles. "May I come in?" he asks, the picture of a southern gentleman.

I step to the side and hold out my arm, "Mi casa es su casa, hermano."

"Glad to see you're still hanging onto that sense of humor, baby sister." He stops and gives me a side hug on his way in. He sets everything but a bottle of water on the desk, then walks over and sinks to one knee in front of Faith. "How are you holding up?" he asks her gently.

"I'm okay," she says shakily, but she doesn't meet his eyes.

Teddy reaches out and lifts her wrist to his eye level, "I didn't hurt you back there, did I?"

She looks up with surprise, "No, I'm fine. You don't have to worry about me."

Teddy turns around to me, "Sadie, would you give us a few minutes of privacy? Patrick and Glitch are down the hall getting more sandwiches together, if you wouldn't mind joining them."

I glance at Faith, but she doesn't send any 'rescue me' vibes, "Sure, Teddy. Take your time." I shut the door with a quiet click behind me as I exit.

NINE
UP IN SMOKE

I walk silently down the hall towards the light, which I see is coming from a small industrial-looking kitchen. I hear voices as I approach, and pause for a moment just out of sight. It's Glitch speaking.

"I'm just saying, you know the captain is going to be pissed you didn't follow orders and escort them straight to the dollhouse. Is this girl really worth getting reprimanded over?"

"Glitch, you've made your point. But what was I supposed to do, let her get kidnapped? You know what they would have done with her, and I'm telling you, I can live with a reprimand, but I couldn't live with that." Patrick sounds frustrated.

"I mean, I know she's the first Polymorph they've found, but I am just saying, I personally don't see what the big deal is. The population is continuing. Sure, the quarterly population reports weren't great. But as long as the program is working, who cares that she's some genetic unicorn? She's got six brothers. If something happens to her, they can rope them all in and get sperm samples. Bing, bang, boom."

I let out a small gasp and it feels like my blood runs cold. I'm not one hundred percent sure what they're talking about, but I'm the only girl here with six brothers. Heck, I'm the only person I've met *ever* with six brothers. The idea of them all getting dragged into this god-awful system because there's something weird about my genes is the absolute worst thing I can imagine. My family is not some guinea pig jackpot for this stupid, soul-sucking eligibility pool. It's bad enough that they've got Teddy, I will not let them drag any of my other brothers into this, no matter what it takes.

There is a clatter, and footsteps briskly head towards the doorway. I straighten just as Patrick rounds the doorway and almost flattens me. He shoots out a hand and steadies my shoulder, "Sadie! Are you okay? How long have you been out here?" He glares pointedly over his shoulder at Glitch as he walks up.

"Uh, hey there Sadie. This isn't awkward at all. Didn't Teddy bring you your sandwich? When is he coming back, by the way?" He tugs at one of his sleeves, clearly a nervous habit.

"So, which one of you jerks is going to tell me what the heck a polymorph is, and what this program wants with my brothers?" I ask angrily, without beating around the bush.

Glitch freezes, "Heh, funny, where did you hear about a polymorph? It's such a funny word, I mean, who even knows what that is, or why it would be significant?"

Patrick groans, "Dude, this is your fault. And you have NO chill. Sadie, come on in and we'll get you something to eat and explain, I promise." He gestures into the kitchen, where I can see that they were assembling what appear to be grilled cheese sandwiches. My stomach growls loudly, evidence that I never got that second bite of pasta at dinner. I walk over to one of the tall stools next to the metal prep counter, and take a seat. Patrick comes over and holds out a soda and a bottle of water, and I take the water.

It's hard to feel confident wearing a too-big guard's uniform, but this is a fake-it-till-you-make it situation from top to bottom, "Somebody better start talking, because I'm feeling straight out of patience."

Glitch swallows nervously, and looks at Patrick, "Are you sure you want her to know? We could get in major trouble if it gets out we told her. Like, re-posted to the middle of nowhere, Nunavland Territories and wearing a parka to pee, trouble."

Patrick looks me in the eyes, and says calmly, "We can trust her. She won't tell anyone else." I feel like he's extending an olive branch, which I appreciate.

"Okay, well, then, a polymorph is a type of genetic difference. Well, technically it is also used in biology, technology, chemistry, and a whole host of different fields that really—" Glitch begins, before being abruptly cut off.

"Glitch, man, get to the point," Patrick urges.

"Right! Sorry. A polymorph for the purposes of this discussion is a person whose genes have a variant, which means the Sterilization Vector was unable to impact them. Whether that happened over time, or your family has never been impacted, we don't know. All we know is that your genes are clean. No Sterilization effects, no sign of any reproductive issues. Just, one hundred percent, grade-A human woman." He rambles to a sudden stop. "They're calling you *the* Polymorph because, well, you're the first one they've found since the first generation post-Sterilization."

I let that sink in for a minute, trying to process what he's just said. "Is that why I have so many matches? In one of the training classes the nurse mentioned that the program's record so far was four, but I have seven."

"Actually," Glitch seems fired up, "You have more than seven! Those seven were just the top choices. As a polymorph, you could technically reproduce with any man who isn't completely sterile himself."

Patrick looks sideways at him for that addition, and I lean back on my bar stool. "Wait, are you saying . . . Are you saying I don't even need to be in this program? I could marry anyone, and I could have kids and just be, well, normal?"

"Well," he looks thoughtful, "Most men are still of relatively limited fertility at this point in the genetic recovery. But, as long as your chosen man was willing to get himself tested and was at least, oh, I don't know, twenty-five percent or better sperm counts, yeah, you could have a baby with him. If he's better than fifty percent you guys would probably have seven or more kids of your own."

My mind is reeling. I don't need to be in this program. I'm normal? Like truly, reproductively *normal.* "Why wasn't I told any of this? If that's true, I don't need to marry any of these men! I can go home and marry whoever I want and still meet the reproduction guideline."

Glitch looks at Patrick and shoves his glasses further up on his nose, a nervous expression taking over.

Patrick answers this time, "Well, as you know the program became mandatory several years ago, for everyone."

I snort, "Don't you mean, everyone with a uterus? Men have the choice to opt out."

"To a degree; they do still have to give sperm and pretty much give up on any chance of marriage and raising kids of their own. It's not without cost to either side of the equation."

"Sure, but I'd *love* to have that choice. I think we all know the human race is in trouble, but it doesn't mean that women everywhere want to be sacrificial lambs to save it!" I can hear myself getting louder, and try to rein it in. It's hard, though. He doesn't understand, and he probably never will.

"I'm not saying it's right. I'm just saying it's . . . what it is, right now." He looks sympathetic, which irks me even more.

I decide to change the subject for now to another point Glitch made, "So, if I'm a match for pretty much anyone, how did I end up with the seven I was assigned?"

"Oh, that's really simple!" Glitch is back in teacher mode and pulls a mini-tablet out of his pocket, "If you pull up your Bachelor Book, you'll see that those seven were the highest candidates in fertility as well as some combination of rank, wealth, or some special status that gives them priority for female complements with the highest fertility." He clicks around the screen a few times before handing it to me, and a completely different version of the Bachelor Book is open.

Right up front I see my seven matches listed, and each of them has a rank listing of *one* in at least one category that he mentioned. "These guys don't all have very high fertility ratings. In fact, the only one over eighty percent is . . . oh." I blush. Patrick. He's busied himself crisping the first grilled cheese, so mercifully his back is to me, and he doesn't see it. "If their fertility scores aren't all that high, how did they get matched with me? Shouldn't I be matched with someone genetically similar? That's the whole premise of this program."

"In theory, yes, but again, these are some of the wealthiest, most powerful men in the world. So they paid top dollar to be given the highest rank. I'm pretty sure Patrick was the only one you got assigned solely based on genetic compatibility, the rest paid to be top of the list for a wife with over sixty percent fertility ratings." Patrick stiffens at that admission, but just keeps flipping sandwiches

My jaw drops, "Wait just a cotton-picking minute, what do you mean they *paid* for a top rank? How is that even possible?"

Glitch doesn't seem to process my instant fury, and continues rattling his answers off nonchalantly, "Oh, men have been paying for priority rankings since the beginning. That's how all of the New Life Centers were funded and staffed to begin with. Most of them are from less genetically-healed families and have no siblings or blood relatives to leave their companies and fortunes to without the program finding them a suitable wife. So, those men typically place a hefty initial donation, and sign a contract which promises a ten percent lifetime royalty into the program after the birth of their first biological child."

The implications of what he just said so casually are slowly sinking in. I am here, sitting in this compound where potential kidnappers tried to steal me less than an hour ago, and it's all so some rich SOB can pay the government to have me as his own, personal broodmare? Oh, excuse me, what was it they called us? Dolls. Just lifeless playthings, to be moved around as they please.

I want to scream. Physically, literally, scream so loud I shatter every window in this place. But I don't . . . because all that would do is hurt my throat. Instead I shove it down and make a vow to myself, that no matter what, I will get out of this. I will come out on the other side, not just alive, but swinging. And heaven help anyone who tries to stop me.

Patrick turns around with a steaming sandwich on a plate, which he slides in front of me. I look up from the crisp, golden crust to his concerned gaze. He doesn't say anything, and neither do I, but when his expression changes from concern to hard calculation, I know he can see the fire blazing in my eyes. I'll burn this program to the ground before I'm through. One way or another, they are going to pay for doing this to me, to us all.

I pick up my sandwich and take a bite. "Thank you, it's delicious."

TEN

THE DATING GAME

The rest of last night passed without incident. After we ate our sandwiches, I excused myself back to our borrowed room, kicked Teddy out, and Faith and I went to bed . . . in Guff and Sweet's beds, but bed nonetheless. It felt like I stared at the ceiling for hours, with the anger at the corruption of this program burning in my gut. I must have turned over a hundred ideas on how to change things, how to rip this unjust place apart at the seams, but when it all comes down to it, I have no power; no influence, no money to speak of, and no control over myself—let alone the people in charge of this place. I am going to change this one day, but unfortunately for now I'm stuck. I made myself a promise, though. A promise to keep my head down, and find a way once I'm on the other side of this to make this right for the girls coming up behind me.

Sometime during the night, the cleanup crew disposed of at least one body, and cleared the grounds of the other would-be kidnappers. Or at least, that's what we were told when we came out of our room for breakfast. Someone delivered fresh clothes for Faith and me, so we're dressed and heading back to the dormitory to do whatever they tell us next. What's next remains to be seen, since all of our training has been on reproductive basics and infant care.

Patrick drops us off at the front door with a brief nod, and then walks briskly down the driveway towards the guard shack, as he called it. His watch has alerted him several times on the way over that the security team is meeting to review last night's events, and how to "tighten up," whatever that means. We let ourselves in, and head to the sitting room to see who else is up.

Everyone is there, except Margaret and Charlotte. Several of the girls jump up and rush to hug us as soon as they spot us.

"We were so worried about you! How did you get separated from everyone else? Are you okay? Where have you been all night?" Beth-Ann is barely breathing, as she rapid-fires questions at us one after the other.

"We're fine, Beth-Ann. We spent the night in the staff quarters, on lockdown just like you guys were. We were just closer to the back exit of the building than the front, so that's where they took us." I omit the details about Glitch's creative re-routing, because the end result is the same.

Elena interjects next, "Be glad you went the back way! It was so frightening, there were at least five kidnappers out there between us and the dorms. The guards surrounded us and we had to all huddle together as they moved us across the lawn and into the house with these big black shields. We didn't see anything but we heard more than one gunshot! It was so scary!" She ends in a rush. Faith gives her a comforting hug, but doesn't mention our own run-in with a kidnapper.

"I'm just glad we're all safe," Faith says soothingly.

"Yeah, thanks to Atlas!" Josephine says. "He ran ahead to the door and started barking orders at the guards like he owned them or something. They didn't even argue, just grabbed the shields from somewhere and formed up around us. He stayed right at the front, and then barricaded himself in with us until the cleanup crew was done. Total hottie." She fans herself.

I can't help but ask, "Who's Atlas?"

"UGH!" Josephine snarls, "Freaking lucky Nell got matched with him. Why does she get Mr. Muscle Mountain and I get friggin' *Elijah*!" She spits his name like it's a cuss word.

I glance over at Nell, who's looking rather pale at the mention of her match. She doesn't seem quite so enamored of him as Jo is.

Jenna pipes up, "Plus, don't forget, everyone isn't exactly safe and sound." She looks guiltily at Leigh. "Marcus and Randy both got bullet grazes following us to the dorms. It was pretty crazy out there; it's a miracle more people didn't get hurt."

Jo snorts, "Sure, a miracle named Atlas. He saved all of our bacon last night. I'm not saying I'm a big fan of this whole system, but I'll be danged if I'm going to volunteer to take off with people who try to snatch us in the black of night. At least the program has rules, and we'll eventually get to move on with our lives when we're through. Who knows why the heck they wanted us, anyways? It's not like there aren't women outside this property who'd be easier to grab."

I decide to change the subject, "Hey guys, where are Charlotte and Margaret? Are they okay?" Then I look at Beth-Ann, "Also, are you married now?"

She chuckles, "Well, it looks I'm a blushing virgin for another day. Due to the attack last night, our wedding was postponed to tomorrow afternoon. And, yeah, Margaret and Charlotte are fine. Margaret's upstairs. Charlotte and her fellas were put on a high-speed train this morning heading to York."

"Oh, no. I didn't even get to say goodbye." I'm genuinely upset by that, as I know she wasn't looking forward to going for whatever procedure they needed to do on her.

"They didn't waste any time loading them up this morning, that's for sure," Elena agrees. "Don't worry, though, we all gave her extra hugs from you two."

She's such a sweetheart. And moments like these it hits me how young she is. I don't have long to brood on it before a message lights up the TV screen hanging on the wall.

Please meet in the main assembly hall for instructions on the next phase of the matching process at your earliest convenience.

Oh joy. "Somebody should go grab Margaret," I say, voice flat.

"Welcome back, ladies!" Eric booms from the front of the room, "I hope you're all well-rested after last evening's kerfuffle!" He looks around with his signature toothpaste-ad grin, but we're all subdued this morning. "Ah, yes. It is regrettable that your first meeting with your matches was interrupted, but it's time to forget all that, and move on to the next phase. The dating phase!" He pauses, as if to wait for applause, but none is forthcoming. "This is the most fun you will have until your honeymoons begin, and for most of you it's a pretty simple process. You and your match will have the opportunity to schedule a nearly endless variety of dates over the coming weeks, designed specifically to help you get to know one another, and grow closer as a soon-to-be married couple." He gives us a self-assured smile.

For those of you with more than one match, you will have to choose which match or matches you'd like to involve in each activity, but it's recommended that you not go more than seventy-two hours without seeing a match, unless you're ready to let him go back into the pool. When you are ready to release someone, you can do it from your mini-tablet, right in the Bachelor Book app—which, by the way, has been updated to show each of you only your perfect matches, and give you additional details about their lives and histories."

"Due to the *issues* last night, the program director has also decided to bring in a slightly heavier guard presence than you ladies have seen up until now. Remember, they are only here for your protection. You have nothing to fear as long as you're within the New Life Center's grounds. Now, does anyone have any questions? No? Fantastic." He wanders off, without waiting for any of us to respond this time.

I reach into my jeans pocket, and pull out the mini-tablet. Yep, there's a notification on the Bachelor Book. I tap it and, sure enough, my seven matches are listed, but there's nowhere near as much information about them as Glitch's version showed me. No ranking, no match or fertility percentages, just basic bio data. Why are they not showing us information that could help us make an informed decision? I mean, if a guy is half as fertile as the another, the woman deserves to know that, especially if it's the difference between being forcibly divorced and moved multiple times, like Faith has been, or getting it right on the first try.

I close it, and see that a new app has popped up on the home screen, which will allow me to schedule "dates" with the various men. I shove it back into my pocket and look around, and see that everyone else is still looking at theirs.

Elena squeals with excitement, "Ooh! Look, Leigh, we can do double dates! What do you want to do first?"

Leigh looks slightly less enthused, "Well, I should probably pick two so I can go for one with each man. Uhm . . . do you mind going on both with me? So you can tell me who you like better?"

"Of course, girl! How about . . . bowling? Who do you want to bowl with? And let's make a dinner reservation for the other one. Hopefully we actually get to eat the dinner this time." She rolls her eyes dramatically.

Beth-Ann takes me in, standing with my hands in my back pockets instead of jumping into the dating frenzy with everyone else. "You have seven guys to pick from, and you don't look excited to schedule a date with any of them. What's up with that?"

I sigh. "I know I need to bite the bullet and just do it, but, it's overwhelming. I mean, there are seven of them and only one of me. Plus, most of them aren't from here. That means I could be dragging someone away from their home, or they're going to drag me away from mine."

"Hey, don't worry about that yet. Just schedule an outing with each of them, spend a little time getting to know them individually, and then send home anyone you still have no sparks with," she suggests.

"What if I don't have sparks with *any* of them?" I'm not trying to be difficult, I'm just worried. I've had a case or two of childhood butterflies, but that's it. None of the boys back home ever made me think about settling down, or heck, even sneaking off to go make out somewhere. Of course, most of them weren't brave enough to get past the brother barrage to even try.

I pull the tablet back out. Okay, planning dates. Here goes nothing. I open the scheduling app, and see that there is a list of suggested activities on the first page. Top of the list, horseback riding. I perk up a little; they've clearly taken my preferences into account, which is helpful. I see that they've even recommended two men for the activity: Asher the veterinarian, and Grant the rancher. Makes sense, they both love animals. Today seems like the perfect day to go meet the horses in daylight, so I accept those date suggestions.

It dings, telling me my first date is in half an hour, and the next one an hour after that.

"Okay, Beth-Ann, I'm going to ride horses with a couple of bachelors. Wish me luck!" I say, feeling happy at least about getting to ride a horse, even if it's not Morgan.

I arrive at the big white barn with ten minutes to spare, so I decide to wander the aisle and introduce myself to the horses. I walk in the big main doors and am immediately surrounded by the smell of hay and warmth. God, there's nothing as good as that clean hay and horse scent. Somebody should make that into a candle, they'd make a fortune. As I come up to the first stall, I cluck softly, and a warm brown nose appears over the half-door.

"Hey, buddy, nice to meet you. I'm Sadie. What's your name?" I look around for a name plate, and spot it to the right. Doc. That's cute. He whuffles my fingers softly. "Hey, Doc, you're a real sweetie. Maybe we'll go for a ride soon, okay?" I give his nose a gentle rub before moving on to the next horse. I make my way past Bullet, Daisy, and Champ before I spot a treat dispenser at the end of the aisle. I quickly stuff my pockets, and continue making my rounds. Hercules, Maggie, and Angel are all big fans of the little biscuits. I walk up to the last stall, and see a pretty Palomino stick his head over.

"Hey bud, what's your name?" I'm in much better spirits already, and I haven't even touched a saddle. I spot his name, and can't help but laugh. "Twinkie? Well you must be a real character to get a name like Twinkie. Although, I guess the coloring fits, huh?" I palm a biscuit and offer it to him, and he snatches it greedily. This guy actually closes his eyes for a second as he chews. "You're a real food lover, I see. I can't say I blame you—I never turn down good grub myself." I give him a little scratch under his forelock, and his head bobs low with appreciation.

I hear a set of boots approaching, but I just keep scratching Twinkie in his favorite spot until someone speaks, "Excuse me, are you Miss Sadie?" I turn and see a young uniformed man, who looks to be in his late teens or early twenties.

"You can just call me Sadie. Are you a groom here?" I ask with a smile.

He nods, "Yes, I am. I'm Michael. Can I saddle him up for you? Or, actually, we usually recommend Angel for the ladies until you get more comfortable. Did you see Angel? She's the nice white mare over there." He points across the aisle.

"I did see Miss Angel, and she is very sweet. But I think I'd like to take out Hercules today, if that's all right." I'd instantly fallen in love with the big dapple gray. He seemed feisty, and we clicked right off the bat.

Michael looks unsure, "Uhm, well, technically there's no rule against it, but I'll have to clear you in the round pen before I can let you take him out alone. Unless you want me to come on your date? Because he's a more advanced mount. We used to be able to let you pick whoever, but we had a few of the bachelors fall last year, and now we have to clear you before you can take anybody but Angel, Doc, or Champ."

"That's no problem Michael, you can clear me in the round pen if you need to. If you'll point me to his saddle I'll get him tacked up in a jiffy." I say politely.

"Oh, I can saddle him for you, miss. It's no trouble at all; that's my job." He starts walking towards the tack room, and I follow.

"I'm sure you can, but I like to saddle my own horse. I feel like it builds the connection, you know? I like to give a horse my attention before I demand something from him.It's a two-way relationship." We walk into the tack room, and he goes for an

English setup. "Uh, Michael, if it's all the same to you, I'd prefer a western saddle. Is there one that fits Hercules?"

"Sure, each horse has a few sets of tack." He turns and grabs the saddle above, and I reach over and pick up the bridle from the hook next to it. "So, I take it you already know how to ride," he says with a wry expression.

"Yep. My family runs cattle down in Jackson Flats. I've been riding my whole life." It's nice talking to someone who doesn't have any agenda, just shooting the breeze. It feels like it's been an eternity, even though I've only been here a week.

"That's cool. I learned from working here. But, uh, I still have to watch you saddle up and check everything the first few times. Sorry, it's policy." He looks sheepish.

"I understand, we have to keep these guys safe."

Back at Hercules's stall, he sets the saddle down on a stand. "I'll be right back with a brush kit. They were all groomed this morning, but Herc's a roller."

I see what he means; there's straw stuck to his back and mane. He hurries back with a tub of brushes, and we each go to work on a side. Hercules seems to enjoy the attention, and props his back hoof. We've got him shined up after a minute, and I grab the pad and saddle.

"Are you sure you don't need help? That saddle's pretty heavy, and I really don't mind," Michael offers again.

"Nope, just stand back—I don't want to clip you with a stirrup." I quickly arrange the girth strap and stirrup, then give it a swing and gently settle the whole setup on Hercules's back. He snaps his ears forward, clearly interested in what comes next. I scratch his shoulder, then under his ribs as I reach for the girth. He stamps a hoof once it's tightened, as if to say, "Let's go already!" Michael hands me the bridle, and I flip the reins over the horse's head, which he lowers amicably for me to slip the bridle over. He's not a complete pushover, though—I have to wiggle my finger at the corner of his mouth before he lets me pop the snaffle bit in. I get it settled, fix his forelock, and give him a little cheek scratch.

"Ready boy? My date should be here in a minute, maybe we can go knock out this round pen thing while we wait." I turn to ask Michael and see that I've already got a date audience. "Oh, Grant! I didn't see you there."

He's leaning casually against a post, in well-worn jeans and boots that I can tell have seen some hard work. His flannel shirt is rolled up to his elbows, showing off his nicely muscled forearms. He has a genuine smile for me. "I was coming to see if you needed help, but I can tell you've got it handled."

"Oh, yeah, I've been doing this since I was tall enough to reach," I agree.

"I can tell. Well, sir, any recommendations on who I should take out today?" He addresses Michael this time.

"Unless you choose Angel, Doc, or Champ I'll have to clear you in the round pen or come with you on your date," he states matter-of-factly.

"Let's say I want somebody with more spunk. Who would you recommend?" he prompts.

He looks thoughtful, "For someone of your height, Bullet is probably your best bet. I'll go get his saddle." He heads back to the tack room.

"He seems to be a good guy," Grant observes. "You can tell he cares about the horses."

"Yes, he's been really nice," I agree. I'm starting to feel nervous, despite the horse magic woven into the air. This is as close to my home turf as I can get, I remind myself. I'm on solid ground here.

Grant and Michael saddle up Bullet in a jif, and I give out cookies to the first horses I greeted before I found the dispenser.

After demonstrating to Michael that we can both stop, turn, walk, and trot our horses in the round pen, he hands Grant a small radio which clips to the back of the saddle, in case we need assistance. We're released to pick a trail, so we choose a green marker, and then it's just us and the horses, walking in the cool shade of the woods. For a few moments, it's just quiet and I soak in the peaceful familiarity hungrily. The land has more of a roll to it here than it does back home, but I relish feeling that connection that I've so missed.

Grant is the first one to speak, "So, we got interrupted that first night, and didn't get to talk much about where we're from or our families. I know y'all run cattle, and you have six older brothers, but that's about it. What else do I need to know about Sadie Taylor?"

Where to even start? "Well, I'm nineteen, so I'm a later entry to the program." He nods, and I keep trying to think of something he'll find interesting, "My parents were high school sweethearts, and all of my brothers but two were old enough that they didn't have to participate in the marriage program. Cade's twenty-six, and he opted out last year. Teddy you saw at the meet-and-greet dinner; he got matched to Faith. Our land has been in my family for four generations now—my brothers and I are the fifth."

"It's nearly unheard of these days to have such a large family —your parents have truly been blessed." He sounds sincere, "Do you guys raise anything other than cattle?"

"No, not much for sale. We breed the horses every few years when we want a new batch of colts, and we have a garden for our own use. Oh, and my dad plants a big flower patch for my mom every year, since she loves fresh flowers so much. She shares those with the ladies at church," I finish. That's probably more detail than he wanted, but I'm not sure where the line is with him. He seems interested, at least. "What about you, do you raise more than cattle?"

He chuckles, "Yeah, you could say that. We do cattle, of course. We've got a few hundred head of Brangus. We also have horse and livestock guardian dog breeding programs, plus our exotics."

Now I'm curious, "What kind of exotics do you have?"

"Well, we've actually got quite a few now. We've got ostrich, emu, several different types of non-native deer, a small wolf pack, and even a couple of big cats." He directs Bullet around a log, and I follow with Hercules.

"How on God's green earth did you go from a rancher to a full-on zoo?" I've never heard of a ranch with that many exotic animals.

"It's kind of a long story. But, the gist of it is, a few years before I took over from my pops, the ranch fell on hard times. We had a couple of real dry years, and with no grass the herd almost ate us out of house and home, and the town was close to being closed." He scoots Bullet back to the side of the trail, so I can bring Hercules back up to his side. "We were close to the whole place going under, when an old school friend of mine called me up. He had left town to become a closer, and a city they were working in a few hours away had a bird sanctuary that had been abandoned. Luckily it was large, and the birds foraged for food and survived. He asked if I could make room for some ostriches, and paid me a good fee to come pick them up and give them a home at the ranch."

I knew closers were tasked with cleaning up and shuttering abandoned towns, but I never dreamed they'd find abandoned ostriches. "That's crazy! So, you just stuck them in a field? They're fine?"

"We've had to build specialty fencing and create separate areas for each new species, but yeah, overall they're pretty happy. They each have a good-sized shelter and plenty of room to roam. Plus, you've never seen anything funnier than a whole flock of ostriches chasing the feed buggy." he snorts in amusement.

I laugh, taken by the mental picture. "I can only imagine! So how's the ranch doing now?" I'm thinking back, and I'm pretty sure Glitch's Bachelor Book had his wealth listed in the mid-seven figure range. Something had to have turned around.

"It's doing great. That was a real turning point for our ranch and our whole town, really. It became a regular thing. Now I employ several young men in town as a road crew to pick up new acquisitions when the closers find them, and transport them to us, or other sites like ours if it's a species we aren't able to keep. They've done pickups from Playa Reino all the way up to Ionoiri, so far." He sounds proud, and he should be. It's impressive that he was able to save his ranch, and the town.

"That's amazing. I know so many places have closed up and had to consolidate. Jackson Flats is really the only decent-sized city for a few hours in any direction, now. Everything else is either closed or abandoned." It's crazy to drive to the nearest city, and pass so many ghost towns. Some of them were closed by a team and look like they could reopen at any minute. Others have been abandoned far longer, and nature is starting to take back over.

We ride and chat amicably, and before we know it, the green trail markers have led us back to the stable grounds. We dismount and lead the horses towards the door. Michael appears, and takes the reins from us. "It's okay,Michael, I'd really like to brush him down," I try to argue.

"I'm sorry, Miss, your next date is already here picking a horse. I thought you might like to take Twinkie out next, so I've already got him saddled for you," he says before leading away Hercules. I guess I'll have to visit him for one last scratch after my next ride. I look awkwardly at Grant, not sure how to end this and just ride off with my next date.

He saves me from my floundering, "I had a great time riding with you today, Sadie, and I hope we can do it again real soon. I know you have a few other fellas to attend to, but I'd love to join you for any meals you are willing to share in the meantime."

I smile at him, "I enjoyed it very much, too, and I'd love to share a meal with you! I'll see what we can schedule." I feel like I should at least try to give him a side hug or something, so I take a step forward. Before I make contact, he's already taking a step back. He tips his hat, seeming oblivious to my attempted hug, and heads off down the path.

I watch him go, but I'm confused. It's nice to know that he isn't going to push the physical intimacy, but I didn't think a hug would hurt. *That's something I can worry about later.* I blow out a breath. I guess it's time for round two. I head into the barn, and see Asher standing next to Michael and Doc, who's saddled up and ready to go.

"Hi, Asher. Thank you for agreeing to come riding with me today." I shove my hands in my back pockets.

He steps towards me, but stops as Doc follows him. "Of course. Thank you for thinking of me. I don't get to do a lot of riding, but I always enjoy it when I have the opportunity."

That's interesting. I wonder if he works a lot? "Well, we've got some time now at least. The trails are very nice here."

Michael walks up, leading Twinkie. "I saw you guys head down the green trail. If you're up for a little longer ride, blue takes about fifteen minutes more but leads to a lake with a picnic area. I could call and have lunch waiting for you, if you'd like."

"That sounds great, Michael, thank you!" Asher sounds pleased. He turns to me, "Ready to go?"

"Yes, let's go find this lake!" We lead the horses out and mount up. I give Michael a wave, and we head off towards the blue trail marker.

"So, how was your morning?" Asher asks once we're on the trail, riding side by side.

"It was good. This has been my first chance to make it to the barn and go riding. Well, in the daylight, anyways," I add.

"What do you mean, in the daylight?" He looks confused.

"Uh, well, when the attack happened, Patrick and Teddy escorted us out the back, and we hid briefly In the barn before heading to the staff quarters where we waited it out for the night." I explain. It hits me that I haven't spoken to him since, and I didn't even ask him what happened to them. Or Grant, for that matter, although he'd seemed fine. "What happened to all of you? You weren't hurt, were you?"

"No, we're all fine. The guards swarmed us so quickly, we didn't see where you'd gone. They split us into two groups, and took most of the men to our dormitory. After that it was just waiting to hear they'd cleared the grounds, and that you were safe."

I feel a sting of guilt. I hadn't asked if all of my matches were safe, and to be honest it hadn't even crossed my mind until now. I feel like an awful person; one of these men is supposed to be my husband, and I didn't even care if they were shot at. *This cannot be a good start to a marriage.* Keeping those thoughts to myself, I respond as honestly as I can, "Well, I'm glad that you're all safe and everyone's in one piece. It was a scary night for all of us, I think."

We fall silent, and the horses walk along happily, unaware of the human drama going on around them. Twinkie keeps trying to steal nibbles off the plants we pass, but I keep him in line for the most part. It's not uncomfortable silence, but eventually he breaks it again.

"Do you have any questions about me, or my day to day life that I can answer?" he asks.

My face heats. He really shouldn't have to ask me; I should know to ask him. "Of course! Yes. I know you're a veterinarian. What kind of animals do you treat?"

"I treat a little bit of everything. The fewer veterinarians there are, the more we see. I am the only vet for several hundred miles in my territory, so I stay busy and I never know what will come through my door." He looks relaxed on Doc's back, one hand resting on the saddle horn with the reins. There's a slight breeze playing with his dark hair.

"That's so cool! I used to want to be a veterinarian when I was a little girl. One of my favorite calves got sick, and didn't make it. And I thought that a veterinarian was like a superhero —if I'd been one I could have swooped in and saved that little calf." I trail off.

He gives me a warm smile, "That's cute. I bet you'd be a great vet. You have an excellent way with the horses."

It's nice that he noticed. "What about family? Who is waiting for you up north?" He didn't mention any family, although we hadn't had much time to talk before.

"No one, really. My mother moved further south several years back, when the winters got too hard on her, and my father died several years ago. I don't have any siblings," he states flatly.

"I'm sorry. That must be lonely. Do you at least have some good friends in Saskerta?" I can't imagine having so little family around. Who does he eat with on the holidays?

He shrugs, "It can be lonely, especially in the winter when people aren't out much. But I stay so busy, I don't have much time for a social life. Plus, my clients are great people, and I get to see them every day." The trail we're following opens to a pretty clearing, and I see the sparkling blue lake beyond it. This place could be on a postcard.

Over to the left, a brightly striped, yellow blanket is laid out under an oak tree, and I see a basket and two place settings. There's even a wooden hitching post, and a water trough for the horses a few paces away. It seems they've thought of everything. "This looks really nice!" I compliment the setup.

We tie off the horses so they can reach the water if they get thirsty, and then make our way across to the picnic that's been set for us. Asher starts distributing napkins and silverware from where they were set neatly to the side, and I open the basket to see what they've brought us for lunch. Inside I find fresh yeast rolls, a paper bag full of fried chicken that's still steaming hot, as well as pasta salad, fresh cut fruit, and an assortment of cheeses. There's even a bottle of wine, but I just set that to the side. We each choose from the abundant selection, and then get settled next to each other, facing the lake.

"Sadie, I hate to ruin a perfect day, but I need to be frank with you," Asher says after a moment.

That sounds ominous. "Uhm, okay. Is something wrong?" I ask tentatively.

"No, nothing's wrong. In fact, it's the opposite. You seem very genuine, and you're obviously beautiful, and we're a genetic match. Everything is right. It's just, you have six other suitors. As I was telling you earlier on our ride, I'm the only veterinarian in my area of Saskerta for hundreds of miles. I have to get back as quickly as possible or call my stand-in and let him know he's going to be staying for the long haul. So, I need to know, Sadie, if you would still consider choosing me and moving to Saskerta Territories. I know that you have family here, and some of your matches are local." He pauses, and looks down at his plate. "If you can't see yourself choosing someone who lives so far away, I completely understand. But if that's the case, I just ask that you let me know now, so that I can get back where I'm needed." At that, he looks up and it's my turn to stare at my plate.

I feel a sense of rising panic because I wasn't expecting this at all, especially after how laid-back Grant was this morning. It makes sense that each man would have his own timeline, but I didn't expect to be deciding about someone on the very first date. I don't want to hurt his feelings, but I think I owe him the same honesty he's shown me. I look up to meet his eyes, so warm and open. He is clearly a good man, and someone I could potentially build a life with. I take a deep breath, "Asher, you're so genuine, and I appreciate that about you in the middle of all of this craziness I've been thrown into. Of all the matches I got, you are one that I could see myself being comfortable with and maybe choosing. But you're right," I swallow, "my entire family lives here. Saskerta is such a long way away, that it is not my first choice to move there. I hope you can understand that."

He reaches for my hand and gives me a reassuring squeeze. "I understand completely. When we get back, you can release me from the app. For now, why don't we just enjoy this lunch as two friends, having one perfect day together. Deal?"

I return his squeeze, "Deal." And to my surprise, he doesn't let go of my hand. We finish our lunches there, and talk and make each other laugh, and he never lets go of my hand. It truly is a golden afternoon.

ELEVEN
GO FISH

Releasing Asher back into the eligibility pool was remarkably simple. A few clicks, an "Are you sure?" message, and that was it. An hour later, I saw a shuttle leaving with him in it. I am surprisingly sad to see him go, but I know it was the right decision. I shake my head. There are still six men I need to focus on and narrow down. As soon as I have the thought, my tablet chimes at me. I look down, and see I have a scheduling notification. Three of my matches have requested to join me for dinner, and I have the choice to say yes to all, or yes to each individually. James, Antonio, Matthew. Well, I have to talk to them all at some point, so, yes to all, it is.

For the first time since I've been here, I find myself with a few hours to kill. I've already ridden today, I don't have any meaningful work to do, and all of the other girls are off on dates of their own, so I'm alone in this huge, echoing house. If I were home, I would probably go into the kitchen and bake up a big batch of cookies for my brothers or my parents. Or if it was nearly dinner time, a nice batch of cornbread. Brent especially *loves* my cornbread. It's sweet, and light, and he drowns it in honey every time. The thought sends a pang of sadness straight to my heart. What I wouldn't give for a hug right now.

I try to push the sadness away, as I know none of my family would want me to feel that way. Maybe I'll use the time to write to them, let them know how I am. I grab a notebook from my room, and a pen I brought from home. We have a lovely balcony that I've barely walked on, let alone sat on and enjoyed the cooling weather, so that is where I head to pen some letters. I choose a swing at the end, and try to think of words to describe how it feels to be here. I know I could tell them anything, but it just doesn't feel good to put it down in ink. Once it's there, once I tell them how this is, how can I pull it back? I let out a frustrated groan, and take in the scenery instead. It's really lovely here, and under different circumstances I wouldn't mind coming back here. The lawn rolls gently away to the tree line where the leaves are beginning to color as the weather cools at night. The first hint of orange and yellow is a promise of the beauty that will unfold here in the months before winter takes hold. *I'll probably be married by then.* The thought leaves me feeling sour.

I give up my plans to write letters home, and instead circle back to baking. Maybe I'll go see what they have in the kitchen, and whip something up. It can't hurt, right? With new purpose, I head to my room to put back the notepad and pen. I'm halfway down the length of the porch, when I hear angry voices coming through one of the curtained glass doors. I freeze, unsure whose room it is. Wait, is that *Eric's* voice?

"I get that you don't like your match—he's a pompous prick— but could we please forget about him for now and just try to enjoy our afternoon? We have the place to ourselves—surely you can think of something better to do with our few minutes alone than whine about the inevitable." I can hear the sneer in his normally enthused voice.

I scurry back to my room, slip in, and pull the door to. I'm not sure whose room that was, but it's pretty clear that someone is breaking the "no illegal relationships" rule with Eric. My mind is blown. Who fell for that guy? I mean, he's handsome if you can get past his whole attitude and general over-the-top behavior. But who would be willing to risk getting punished for a relationship with him? The only one who has been remotely close to him is Margaret, and she's frosty to everyone. Surely it's not them. *Could it be them?* I shake that image from my mind and head down to see what baking supplies are available in our kitchen downstairs.

The kitchen, like the rest of the house, is large and well appointed. The white cabinets and flecked beige countertops are sparkling, as if just cleaned. There is a large ranch-style sink, and plenty of room to work. I go over to check out the six burner stainless stove and get excited as I turn it on to preheat. I start opening cabinets, looking for baking supplies. I'm sure they're around here somewhere if they've provided us an entire kitchen. I find a mixing bowl, whisk, and measuring utensils. Now I just need something to put in them. Across from the large island I see a corner door, which I suspect is a small pantry.

It turns out I'm right and wrong, because it is a pantry, but, *wow*, it's enormous. I quickly walk in and find an entire shelving unit of dry goods. I grab up the corn meal, sugar, flour, and leavening. I drop off my haul and head to the refrigerator, which lights up with a large screen as I approach. I see a message scrawled across the screen.

For any additional food needs, feel free to place an order below:

The message is followed by a large open space for writing in requests. I open the door, and see everything I need, except buttermilk. That's okay, I can make do with some lemon juice. I quickly get to work prepping my cornbread, and find myself humming as I work on the familiar task. This is probably the fanciest kitchen I've ever seen; I wonder if anyone has ever made cornbread in it before? They certainly don't serve it at the dining hall, but the menu is kind of generic, clearly meant to please their guests from all over the NAA. Once my cornmeal is soaking in some make-shift buttermilk, I prep a round baking dish, and start measuring up my other ingredients. I methodically finish putting together my corn bread, and slide it into the piping hot oven.

Once the timer is set, I get to work washing up the bowls and utensils. I'm sure there's a dishwasher around here, but I like the repetitive task—it helps clear my head. While I'm washing, I think about my remaining matches, and who I'll see tonight. Now that I know that most of my matches *paid* to be matched with me, considering any of them feels icky. I'm like a modern-day mail order bride, and I don't know how to feel about that. At least with Patrick, he's not cheating the system to be matched; he truly is my best chance to have kids and get out of this program as quickly as possible. He's also local to Georada, although with his career here at the NLC, there wouldn't be much opportunity for him back home. Jackson Flats is primarily a food production town nowadays, filled with ranchers and farmers. Supposedly the site we're on used to be a major metropolitan city that was home to millions. The thought of millions of people living in any one place boggles my mind; I can't remember when I last saw even two hundred people in one place.

I think that no matter what, Patrick has to be one of my top contenders. He's treated me with respect and kindness during the few interactions we've had, and if I wasn't some sort of genetic unicorn, he might be my only match. However, I can't ignore that, for whatever reason, fate has given me options. I told my family I'd do my best to choose wisely, and I will. My ultimate goal is to bring home a man who can truly be a partner and fit into our lives. Someone who will be respectful to my parents and make dumb jokes with my brothers. Someone I can see holding a tiny baby on his shoulder and kissing me on the cheek.

Is that too much to ask, given the state of things? Maybe. Can I bring myself to truly settle for less? I don't know. I guess the worst-case scenario is that in three years, I pack up one or two kids, and head home with a divorce certificate instead of a husband. I think my family will understand if that's how it ends up, and I know they'll adore my kids no matter who their father is. But of the remaining six, who is worth considering? Would any of them help me build the future I want? A partnership, with the chance for love to bloom.

I rinse the last dish and set it on a pristine white towel to dry next to the sink right as the timer goes off. I hurriedly search the drawers for a pot holder—no surprise, it's white—and pull out my perfectly-golden cornbread. The smell of fresh baking washes over me, and I let out a happy sigh. No matter where you are, home cooking can really ground you. I set it aside to cool and check the time. I've got less than an hour until my dinner date, so I'd better go get ready.

I choose a clean pair of jeans, sandals, and a flowy shirt from my closet, before applying some mascara and straightening my hair. I feel a little silly, but if I'm going to be dating these men, I have to give it my all. I am not the kind of person who does anything half-way. Plus, if any of them don't have a spark with me, that will be an easy way to narrow it down.

I head back down the stairs and hear voices coming from the kitchen, so I make my way in there. Nell and Beth-Ann are standing next to my pan of cornbread, debating.

"Well, it didn't appear here out of thin air. We shouldn't cut it without finding out who made it first. What if someone made it for their match? If we cut it, she'll be upset," Nell reasons.

"I don't care who made it, it smells amazing and I'm going to die if I don't have a piece," Beth-Ann argues. *Clearly the pregnancy cravings are hitting her early*, I think with amusement.

I chuckle and they look up. Nell asks, "Do you have any idea where this came from?"

"Yeah, it was me. I had some free time, and I wanted some home cooking. Y'all want a slice?" I offer.

"Yessss!" Beth-Ann practically shouts, and we all start opening drawers until we find the silverware. Once we've all got a slice slathered with butter, she asks, "You weren't planning to deliver this to one of your man-friends, were you?"

I snort, "Nope, not really. Just needed to get my mind off things for a while. I guess I could take them each a piece. I'm meeting three of them for dinner in a few minutes."

Beth-Ann takes a bite and groans loudly, "This is the best thing I've eaten in a week. Maybe longer. Think Phil would mind if I married you instead?"

Nell ignores Beth-Ann and her food love affair, "I'm not sure if I'm jealous that you have so many choices, or feel sorry for you having to deal with it all. Atlas is kind of scary, but at least there aren't six more of him to contend with."

"Atlas, huh? Do you like him? Jo seemed to be a pretty big fan this morning." I say, remembering her look of terror when they were first introduced. I am getting the feeling Nell has had a hard life so far, but I don't want to pry if she isn't ready to share.

She looks hesitant, and takes another bite of her cornbread before answering, "I mean, he's been perfectly civil so far. No red flags or anything."

It's Beth-Ann's turn to snort, "No red flags? What are you expecting, him to come right out and say he sucks as a human?"

Nell looks indignant, "No, of course not! But I trust my gut. And if my gut says I can't trust a man, I stay as far away from him as possible. So far, he seems okay."

"I know what you mean—one of my matches keeps looking at me like a piece of meat. Honestly I'm not sure why—or what to do with James," I admit. "My first instinct was to release him immediately, but I thought it would be rude to not have a single conversation with him first. First impressions can be misleading, right?"

She looks concerned, "Is he one of the ones coming to the dinner tonight?"

I nod, "Honestly at this point I'm glad it's not a one-on-one with him. Speaking of, I should probably head over there." I look at the cornbread, and decide to take it. Can't hurt, right? If a man doesn't like my cornbread I don't think we're destined to be soul mates.

Beth-Ann grabs my arm, "Wait, I need another piece before you take that." She hastily scoops it out, looking triumphant. I just chuckle and make my way to the dining room. The entryway to the main hall is quiet and empty, save one guard who doesn't even look at me as I enter.

The host greets me in a sedate tone, "Good evening, ma'am. Right this way. I believe one of your suitors is already here. What is that you have there?"

I follow him towards the table, "Oh, just some cornbread. I had some free time this afternoon and felt like baking."

"Well, it smells delicious. Could I take that to the kitchen and allow them to plate it for you?"

"Sure, I guess that would be good." I hand over the pan.

We arrive at a table for four and find Matthew already seated. "Here you are, and I hope you enjoy your evening." He walks towards the kitchen with a flourish.

Matthew stands and pulls out a chair for me, "Good evening Sadie, thank you for accepting my dinner invitation."

"Of course. I'm looking forward to an opportunity to get to know you better," I say as I sit.

"The feeling is mutual, especially after we got interrupted at our very first meeting," he states.

Well, he doesn't beat around the bush. That's okay in my book, "Yes, that was quite a night." I decide to take charge for once, unlike my first dates. "So, I'd love to know some of what your expectations are in a wife. Are you looking for someone to move to York? Someone who wants a career or who wants to stay home? Anything I should know about you and your needs?"

He leans back and rubs his jaw lightly. "Excellent questions. I would love someone who was willing to live in York, at least part time. I understand your family is here, and your family business. I'd be willing to work something out where you spend part of the year here, and part of the year in York. I wouldn't expect you to cut ties with your family and never see them again if that's what you're worried about. As far as a career, I'm open to whatever, once the kids are older. There are excellent schools and several industries in York that a woman might find appealing, but if you'd prefer to raise kids and enjoy the finer things in life, I'll make it my mission to provide them for you. As far as my needs, well, everything is negotiable except a commitment. If you're with me, I won't accept anything less than one hundred percent."

Wow, he's really thought about how this could work. I can appreciate that.

He leans forward intently, "What about you, what are your expectations in a husband? Are you expecting someone to move here to Georada and become a cowboy?"

I roll my eyes at his exaggeration, "No, I don't expect anyone to give up his career to become a cowboy. Being close to my family is a high priority, for sure. I hope to find a true partnership, like my parents have. I want to be treated and seen as an equal in the relationship. As far as the finer things in life, I don't need all of that. As long as we are safe and taken care of, the rest is just details."

Matthew looks thoughtful, but before he can say anything else a host brings Antonio and James to the table. James settles himself in the chair next to me while Antonio stops to give me a brief hug. His long brown hair falls forward and he sweeps it back with his hand as he takes the seat across from me.

"How are you, Sadie dahlin'?" Antonio asks, and I am instantly enamored with his Northeastern accent.

"I'm good. How are you, Antonio?"

"Better now that I'm here," he says with a playful grin.

James cuts him a derisive look, "I think we're all happy to be here."

"Down, boy. It's not a contest," Matthew says drily.

James leans forward, crowding into my space, "Really? You don't think this is a contest? What would you call it, then?"

Matthew glances at me and sees me leaning back to try to keep from coming into contact with James's elbow. "I'd call it the beginnings of a relationship, and I think you'd do well to remember that. But, if you can't, more's the better for the rest of us."

I stay silent, not wanting to weigh in on this exchange. I can see more of their personalities coming out now that they're interacting with each other, as opposed to the smooth façade they save for me.

Antonio clears his throat, "So, Sadie, Matthew, what were you discussing before we interrupted?"

Matthew changes gears smoothly, "We were discussing our needs in a spouse. Sadie laid out some really important information. She doesn't expect us to become cowboys, but she'd like to stay close to her family." He gives me a wink.

I can't help but smile back at his charm.

"Sounds about right," I agree, "But also it's extremely important to me to be treated as a partner, and an equal in whatever relationship I choose."

Antonio is intent on my answer, "Those are important things to find in a life mate. How'd you get to be so wise for such a young thing?" he teases.

"Uh, just watching my parents I suppose. They were high school sweethearts, and I've always admired their relationship." I'm not so good at flirting, so they'll just have to accept honesty. I guess it's for the best they know that up front.

"So, what, you've got some romantic fantasy you're clinging to? You do realize that reality is different now than it was then, right?" James says with annoyance.

I look down at my lap, trying to rein in my anger before answering. He must take it as me feeling chastised because he rushes on before I can answer.

"There's more to choosing a spouse than childish whims. A person's career, power, and where they can take you in life are much more significant."

Childish, really? I think angrily, "If you find me so childish, I guess you'll be happy for me to release you back into the eligibility pool. I wouldn't want you to get stuck with me if that's how you feel." I bite out, trying to keep an even tone.

He looks shocked, "Are you serious? Do you have any clue who I am, little girl?" He gets louder, half rising from his seat. "I am the youngest assistant justice in the tri-state, and I'm on track to be the justice before I'm forty! I just need one of you idiots to be my incubator, so I can show voters that I'm a family man!" he seethes.

Antonio and Matthew both stand, and James surges to his feet. I feel frozen, unsure of what to do with him blowing up like this. I briefly consider running to the other side of the table just to have some distance.

"I think you need a little cooling off time, James," Antonio says, hands raised in a reassuring gesture.

"Yes, let's take a little walk." Matthew is less friendly.

"Neither of you have any say in this! I have just as much right to be here with her as either of you!" James's voice is an angry growl.

Seemingly out of nowhere, Patrick appears. "What's with all the commotion, James? You can either calm down or we can take this elsewhere." His arms are crossed menacingly across his chest, showing off the well-defined muscles in his chest.

"I am perfectly calm. I was just explaining to Sadie here," he gestures to where I'm still seated, "that she shouldn't be so hasty to release someone without understanding his background and what kind of life he can provide for her. The seven of us have wildly different means." He looks down his nose at Patrick.

Patrick ignores the obvious jab at him as the only working-class man I'm matched with, "Six of us, you mean. Asher's already headed back to Saskerta Territories."

James whips his head around to me, clearly shocked I had the guts to dismiss someone already. He points a finger at my face, "You listen here, girlie, you might think you're special, because you have so many matches, but you are just another woman. There are nine more of you in this program this week alone. You might get away with sending some back-country vet back to the middle of nowhere-ville, but I am not going to put up with that!"

I have leaned back as far as I can in my chair—bumping into Matthew's leg behind me—to keep James's finger from actually jabbing me, when in the next instant—it's just gone. I snap my head up and see that Patrick has grabbed him by the collar of his suit, and snatched him away from me in one fluid movement. He pulls him up, nose to nose, "I think what you need is a lesson on how to talk to ladies with civility and respect." His voice is eerily calm.

I finally feel my joints unfreeze and jump to my feet, "Patrick, don't do anything to get yourself in trouble! He's not worth it!"

Patrick doesn't loosen his grip, but turns to give me a reassuring look, "Don't worry about me, Sadie. I'm just going to take James here to the captain's office so he can be reminded of the conduct agreement he signed when he applied for this program. Assuming you don't want to spend any more time with him?"

"Definitely not." I say with a shake of my head.

"I'll give you a hand," Matthew says icily.

Patrick and Matthew haul James out by his collar, over his loud protests, "This is ridiculous! I paid good money to be here, and get matched with that spoiled cow!" The door closes behind them, but he can still be heard even from the hallway, "You have no right to put your hands on me, you are nobody, and I will squash you like a bug!" There is a dull sound, and then a loud thump as if someone's fallen to the floor.

I look over with concern at Antonio, and he comes around and clasps my hand between his. "Hey, it's okay dahlin', he's in over his head with those two. Why don't you sit down for a second, and I'll get you some water."

I realize I'm shaking lightly with the feeling of adrenaline pulsing through me, so I take his suggestion and sit back down. He pours a glass of water and presses it into my shaking hands, so I take a small sip. "Incubator? Cow? Dumb child? Is that what you all think of us?" My eyes are beginning to water.

He rushes to disagree, "No! Sadie, that guy is a pompous jerk who thinks way too highly of himself. You are none of those things. You hear me? Not one."

I set my glass of water down carefully, but my heart isn't in this date anymore. Our waiter arrives with a tray containing four elegant plates with slices of my cornbread. He looks pointedly at the vacated seats before setting a piece in front of Antonio and me.

"What's this?" Antonio asks, noting the deviation from the usual bread basket.

The waiter sniffs, "The lady made it for you this evening, I'm sure she'd be delighted to tell you all about it." He turns sharply and leaves us as abruptly as he arrived.

"You made this?" Antonio asks, "What kind of bread is it?"

"You've never had cornbread before, really?" I can't help but chuckle, grateful for the distraction of his confused reaction giving me something else to focus on. *These northerners—what do they even know about good food?*

"No, never. It smells good, though. Is it a fork situation or a "pick it up" situation?" he asks with a hint of excitement.

"However you'd like, but I recommend a hearty slather of butter." I push the butter dish towards him, and he loads it up before taking a big bite off his fork.

He chews contemplatively for a moment, "This is pretty good! It's different, but not bad."

I clasp my hands to my heart, "Not bad? Oh my word. It's my special recipe cornbread and all you can say is 'not bad?'"

He laughs at my dramatics and I give him a warm smile in return.

The rest of our meal passes uneventfully, but Matthew, Patrick, and James never return. When we're finished, Antonio offers to walk me back to the dormitory, which I accept. He places his hand on the small of my back as we walk along the short path in the fading twilight.

"I'll give them one thing, it's beautiful here." I gesture to the scenery.

"It's gorgeous here," he agrees. I turn and see he's looking at me, not the grounds. Blushing, I look down and away.

"Ah, don't get shy on me dahlin'. It's the truth! Will you sit on the porch with me for a while? There's something important I'd like to discuss with you," he says as we ascend the steps to my temporary home.

"Sure, of course. What would you like to talk about?"

He leads me to the swing mounted at the end of the porch, facing more of the verdant rolling hills. "Well, it's something about my past that I think you need to know to make your decision." He pauses, "I'm a father. I have a daughter; she's eleven years old."

"Oh, wow. What's her name?" I'm not sure what else to ask.

"Gianna. She's the light of my life, and everything I do is for her." He smiles in adoration, and I believe him. He holds up a phone and shows me a picture of a beautiful young girl, with rich brown hair and eyes. She's smiling and holding a soccer ball.

"Oh, she's gorgeous!" I exclaim. Then a thought hits me, "If you don't mind my asking, where is her mom?"

His face falls slightly, "Her mother and I were set up by our parents through a matchmaking service, and she died in childbirth from complications. Gianna never got to meet her, but I do my best to keep her memory alive."

I put my hand on his arm to comfort him, "I'm so sorry. That must have been really awful for both of you." I can't imagine growing up without one of my parents, the poor girl.

"It was hard, and I've done my best to give my girl the world. But, you see, she's growing up. Her life is going to go through so many changes in the next few years, and I feel like there are some things that she needs a mother for, you know?"

I nod, "Being a teenager is hard on a girl."

"I'm sure you know that better than I do. I know it's a lot to ask, you being so young and all. But my girl needs someone to be there for her, tell her how to become a good woman. Someone who can answer her questions. Is that something you'd consider?"

He's really putting it on the line for me, and I respect that. But, am I ready to be a mother to an eleven-year-old girl? I don't know the first thing about mothering yet; I always assumed I'd get the benefit of starting with a baby and working my way up. "Thank you for being honest with me," I start, "I don't really know anything about being a mom to an eleven-year-old, which I'm sure isn't a surprise to you."

He's quick to answer, "Of course, you're still young yourself. I just need to know if you're willing to consider it. Give me a shot, give *us* a shot. Family is the most important thing to me, Sadie. My girl, I'd pull the moon down and hand it to her if she asked.

But all she wants is a mother, so I have to try to find her one. I can tell that you're kind, and smart. I'm just asking you to consider this."

In the moment, I'm unsure but I can't kill his hopes. "Okay, I'll consider it. I'm not making any promises, and I'm sure we'll have a lot to discuss. But, we'll keep getting to know each other; give it some time to see if we might be a good fit."

Relief floods his face, "Thank you, Sadie. I won't keep you out here all night." He leans forward and presses a kiss to my forehead before making his way back to the stairs, and disappearing into the night. I sit for a long while, just thinking and staring off into the distance. When it's fully dark, I make my way upstairs and find my tablet. Kicking off my shoes, I drop onto the bench at the end of my bed, and pull up the Bachelor Book app. Six men pop up, all staring into my soul from the screen. I click on Pierce, and invite him to breakfast with me tomorrow morning. Then I select James, and release him back into the pool. *Goodbye, and good riddance. Some other unfortunate woman can be your incubator.*

Twelve

RENDEZVOUS

I take a glorious shower, then slip into my comfiest PJ set. My mom bought it for me for Christmas last year and it has pink bows all over it. I quickly brush my hair, and pull it into a loose braid. Settling down onto the bed, I roll over to check my mini-tablet to see what's scheduled for tomorrow and see a notification alert. I bet it's Pierce, accepting my breakfast invite.

No, it's an ASAP request from Patrick. I sit up, what could he possibly want? Is it about James? I hope he didn't cause more trouble, or what if Patrick needs to tell me I'm somehow in trouble for releasing him? I mean, he was shouting about how important he was, but I didn't learn anything in class about getting in trouble for releasing matches. I frown, and accept the invite. The tablet dings again: Location, front porch. All righty, here I come.

"Oh, shoot, embarrassing pajamas!" I say to no one in particular, looking down at my outfit with regret. I mean, I'm decent. It's just a little embarrassing for someone who I'm trying to build a romantic relationship with to see me covered in tiny pink bows. But, if I stop and change he'll be waiting. "Screw it! I'm going like this!" I grab a long sweater and pull it on as I hustle down the stairs. Thankfully, everyone else seems to already be in their rooms or still out and the sitting area is empty. I stop just inside the front door, and rake my hands through my wet hair towards my braid to try to smooth it. It probably doesn't help, but it makes me feel better.

I open the door, and step out into the darkness. It takes a moment for my eyes to adjust, but then I spot Patrick leaning against the handrail at the bottom of the stairs. Suddenly shy, I am quieter than usual when I greet him, "Hi, Patrick. Is everything okay? James didn't cause more trouble, did he? Am I in trouble?"

He chuckles softly and starts up the steps towards me, "No, of course not. I mean yes, everything is fine. But no, you're not in trouble and James is already on a shuttle home. Between you and me, I think it might get a flat sometime around 3 AM and be held up." His grin is devious. He extends one hand slowly, and catches a tendril of hair in his fingertips before tucking it carefully behind my ear. "How are you doing after all of that earlier?" he asks, stepping closer.

"I'm okay . . . now," I'm caught up in the moment, the heat radiating off of him causes my mind to go blank, and I can't help but stare at his handsome face. He has strong cheekbones, and just a bit of scruff beginning to show along his jawline. His eyes are locked with mine, and it feels like we're completely alone in the world. Just him and me, a boy and a girl, twisted up with electricity.

"You are the most beautiful thing I've ever seen," he says on a quiet exhale.

I can feel my blush creeping up, and I glance down to avoid his deep blue gaze. His fingertips find my chin.

"I mean it, truly. You're stunning in the moonlight. I'll probably dream about kissing you tonight." He locks eyes with me again.

"Just dream?" The words pop out of their own accord; I've never been so bold with a man in my life.

This time the smile spreading across his face is slow, steady. Like the sun peeking up over the horizon in the morning, it shines across his entire face. His hand slides along my jaw to the back of my neck, underneath my braid. He leans in closely, and I think he's going to kiss me right then, but instead he places his lips right next to my ear and whispers softly, "It could be more than a dream, if you're ready."

His lips just barely brush my ear as he speaks, and my whole body shudders. He pulls back just enough to see my face again and waits. It dawns on me that he's waiting for me to give him permission, rather than diving in for the kiss. My heart warms in my chest, and I give him the tiniest of nods.

Without waiting another second, he swoops forward and presses his lips firmly to mine. Warm and strong and firm, yet soft at the same time. It's the most glorious and surprising thing I've ever experienced. He lingers for a moment before pulling back. His thumb glides up and down the side of my neck, and I shiver again.

"Are you cold?" he asks with concern.

"No, I'm perfect," I reply, "But I can't believe I had my first kiss in these ridiculous bow pajamas." I admit sheepishly.

He laughs, loud and surprised before stepping back and taking me in head to toe, "I think they're cute!"

I hang my head in mortification, "They're embarrassing! So, did you just come to kiss me? Not that I'm complaining, I was just worried when I saw the ASAP request." I quickly change the subject, and walk over to the porch railing to lean against it.

He follows and arranges himself next to me, "I'm sorry, I didn't mean to worry you. I just thought you'd like to know that James was already gone, and he wouldn't be bothering you anymore. Plus, I heard some gossip that I missed some homemade baked goods, and I have to admit I was jealous. Do you think I might earn some home baking anytime soon?" He looks hopeful.

Now it's my turn to grin, "What's your favorite?"

"Hmmm," he rubs his chin, "Well, I'm sure anything you make would be good, but I really love chocolate chip cookies. They're simple, but they're my favorite. My mom used to make them as a pick-me-up when I had a hard day at school."

"Aww, that's sweet! Is your mom here in Georada?" I ask and bump my shoulder against his. He hasn't really shared anything about his family so far.

"No, she and my dad live up in Wrightsville now."

"Oh, in the capital? That's pretty far north. How did you end up all the way down here?"

He shrugs lightly, "This is the New Life Center I was assigned to, so here I am."

We're both quiet for a beat.

"Can I ask you something?" He sounds hesitant.

I look up at him, "Of course, what is it?"

"Is there a reason you had a date with everyone except me today? I didn't scare you off the other night, with the kidnapper situation did I?" He looks genuinely concerned.

"Honestly, I haven't thought much about that. Does that make me a bad person? I mean, a man died and I was mostly just relieved to be safe myself. And no, that's not why I didn't ask you on a date. Mostly I just realized I had spent way more time with you than the others, and I didn't want to be unfair and not at least get to finish meeting all of them." I stop abruptly, and decide to omit the part about deciding he was going to be one of my front runners due to his high fertility rating. I wouldn't want him to think I was only after him for his sperm, after all. *Awkward.*

"Ahh, I see," he says, looking down at our feet. "So, does that mean I'm still in the running at least? You're not put off by a lowly security guard?" He gives me a sideways glance.

"Uh, no, definitely not put off by that. You and Grant are the only ones with normal jobs. Everyone else is either fancy or powerful or richer than Solomon. It's a little intimidating, frankly. I'm glad you're just you." I bite my lip, and look away. *He's also the only one I can imagine getting on the floor and playing horse with a little kid. I bet he's going to be a great dad.*

He reaches for my hand, "Well, in that case, would you like to do something with me tomorrow? Rumor is there's a big announcement in the morning, but I'd love to take you riding after if you want?"

He's piqued my curiosity, "What kind of announcement?"

"I have no idea, I just wanted to sneak in a date with you before you have to help Beth-Ann get ready for her wedding," he admits.

I'd completely forgotten about the wedding. *Friend of the year alert.* "Okay, that sounds like a good plan. I would love to go riding, that always helps me clear my head."

He brushes a light kiss against my cheek, right next to my ear before telling me goodnight. He waits for me to head back into the house, and then I hear his steps echo down the porch stairs. It's been a long day, but I can't complain about the ending. I press a hand to my cheek, and head back up to my room.

THIRTEEN
LIGHT THE MATCH

I awake once again to the sounds of windchimes; my days have started to run together in this new pattern. One long stretch, and then I leisurely get dressed and ready to head to my breakfast date. Today it's another pair of jeans, tank top, and a flannel overtop to fend off the nip that's blooming in the air. Hair pulled up in a simple ponytail, I'm ready to face whatever the day throws at me.

Today I run into Leigh in the hallway, we exchange a greeting and fall into step.

She reaches over and links arms with me, "So, how is it going, juggling all those men?" she asks brightly, if a little forced.

"It's definitely not boring. What about you, how are your matches? You had two, right?" I return the question.

She hesitates, "Well, it's okay. Spencer is actually quite handsome, and he's very . . ." her voice trails off, "persistent."

I try to withhold judgment, but knowing what Faith told me about Spencer, it's hard. "Oh yeah? What about your other match?"

Her brow knits up, "He's, uhm, really kind. He seems like a very nice man."

Her tone tells me there's more she's holding back, so I lean against her shoulder, "But?"

"He's so . . . old. Like, he's nineteen years older than me—more than double my age!" She does the math for me.

"Yeah, I could tell he seemed more mature than Spencer," I hedge, really not wanting to steer her either way. I wouldn't be thrilled if my only matches were twice my age or a creepy cold ex-husband to one of my new friends. "What does your gut tell you?"

We are slowly trailing through the entryway, in no hurry to arrive at our destination. She stops, pulls her arm from mine, and starts biting one of her fingernails.

"That bad, huh?" I press. "I won't judge you if you need to talk it out. I'm all ears."

She looks at me anxiously, still worrying her fingernail. "I don't know *what* to think. Spencer is handsome, more handsome than Randy if I'm honest. But he's so pushy. He's tried grabbing my butt twice, and that just makes me really uncomfortable. We went to all the trainings, I know that we have to be physical with one of these guys at some point, but I don't want someone I just met a few days ago grabbing all over me! I thought it would be exciting, and romantic, and . . ." she's starting to tear up, so I pull her into a hug. She grips me tightly in return.

"It's going to be okay. Spencer is acting like a jerk, and he has no right to do anything you're uncomfortable with. Next time he tries something, slap him. Better yet, don't be alone with him to give him any more chance to try something." I pause, unsure how much to say. "Leigh, I think you need to have a talk with Faith."

She pulls back, and shoves her fine strawberry blonde hair back behind her ears, "Faith? Why?"

"I can't tell her story; it's not mine to tell. But, I think if you explain to her about Spencer, she'd be willing to tell you a little bit more about her past, and some things she knows about him." I hope Faith isn't mad at me for telling her that. But we can't let this sixteen-year-old girl go blindly into Spencer's bed —we just can't. He'll chew her up and spit her out sad and broken.

I link arms with her again, and we continue out to the porch.

"Okay, I'll ask." She says quietly.

"Tell me more about Randy. I know he's older, but you said he's kind. What does he do? Is he local?" I change the subject.

She brightens, "His job is pretty cool, actually. He's a closer. So he goes around to all of the cities that have too small a population on their own to sustain themselves, and helps close up everything so that whenever the population increases again, the cities are in good condition. He travels all over the NAA, but his home base can be anywhere he wants. He told me he'd be willing to pick Jackson Flats as his home base, so when we weren't traveling we'd be close to my parents."

"Wow, that's really thoughtful of him! And traveling and seeing the world sounds cool. You'd get to go with him?" I always wondered how that worked. We've made it to the main hall, and let ourselves in the front door. The ever-present guard gives us a curt nod, and we wave back.

"Yeah, he said that any of the guys who are married bring their wives, and sometimes even kids if it's going to be a longer job. There's plenty of room, obviously, so they are allowed to bring them. He's been all the way to the Alaska Territories. Can you believe that? Oh, and he told me some juicy stuff about Calivada, you won't believe what went on over there before the New Lives Program became law."

"What? Now this I've got to hear!" I love seeing how animated she is again.

Before she can tell me the juicy gossip, though, I hear a masculine chuckle to our left. Pierce is standing off to the side, waiting for me to join him for breakfast.

Leigh lets go of my arm, "I'll let you enjoy your date. We'll talk later!" She gives me a wave before walking over to join Elena at a table.

Pierce steps forward and offers his arm, ever the gentleman. I rest my hand on his forearm, and he leads me to a table for two.

Once we're seated and sipping orange juice, he says, "So, I hear you had a rather busy day yesterday. Want to talk about it?"

Oh, boy, I wonder what he's heard? "It was definitely eventful. I don't even know where to begin."

He smiles lightly, "Matthew and Antonio filled me in on having less competition for your affection. I'm sorry James chose to take the low road, though."

I shake my head and look at my lap. "He was a real jerk. I feel sorry for whoever gets matched with him next."

He fidgets with his fork before confessing, "I don't think you'll have to worry about that." My head snaps up. "Matthew spoke with the program director personally, and it sounds like James is being removed from the program entirely. Something about giving the program a bad reputation by throwing around words like 'incubator?'"

I let out a breath I didn't realize I'd been holding, "That's amazing! I'll have to thank Matthew later."

He nods, and our breakfast is delivered by a waiter. We dig in, and the conversation ebbs until I remember something I saw in the Bachelor Book, "So, you're from Calivada, aren't you?"

"Yep, born and raised. That's how I got my start in acting." He looks pleased that I remembered, and I make a mental note to try harder on these dates. I'm never going to dig beneath the surface to find the best match if I don't put in any effort.

"What's it like there? I've never been out of Georada," I confess.

"Really? Would you like to travel one day?" he looks surprised. I nod, and his expression turns thoughtful, "Well, it's an entirely different culture than here on the east coast. We have a really diverse population, especially compared to Georada. There are a lot of different family structures that you probably wouldn't have seen here, and the government is less well-received."

"What do you mean by different family structures? Aren't most non-traditional pairings illegal now?" That's what I've heard, anyways.

He looks uncomfortable, "Uh, yes. Yes they are illegal. However, there are some cities which have rebelled against the government mandates, and they are a lot *freer* with things there. There are whole communities where people have open relationships, and most have multiple partners."

My jaw drops, "Seriously? And everyone's just okay with that?" He's blowing my mind, "Wait, what about the birth rates? Won't those cities eventually just die out when no children are born?"

He quickly glances around the room, and on seeing no one in earshot he leans forward, "Supposedly, their birth rates are even higher than the program. But I wouldn't spread that around if I were you."

My mind is reeling. Is it possible the answer is that simple? Let people be with whoever they want, and things will sort themselves out? "Can I ask, if you think their success rates are as good or better, why are you here planning to marry within the program?"

He looks down guiltily, "Uh, well . . ." He stops, and I can tell he doesn't want to say whatever it is.

"It's okay, you won't hurt my feelings. I'd rather know." I reach across the table and touch his hand in reassurance.

He flips his palm up, and runs his fingers across mine, soft as a whisper. He locks eyes with mine, "How open-minded would you say you are?"

My eyebrows shoot up, that's not what I was expecting him to say, "I don't know, pretty open-minded, I think. Dare I ask why?"

"Take a walk with me?" he asks hopefully. I peruse his handsome, tanned face for a hint of what it is he's hiding, but come up empty.

"Sure. I think we have a few minutes before the mandatory announcement this morning." I set my napkin on the table, and he leads me by the hand out of the dining hall.

We quickly make our way out of the building, and to a stone walking path I haven't seen before. He's still holding my hand, fingers laced lightly together. I wait for him to start the conversation again, as we meander down the path.

He gazes off into the early morning and speaks softly, "I live in one of the communities that is known for its non-traditional relationships." He looks sideways at me, trying to gauge my reaction.

"Ok," I say, waiting for the rest.

He clears his throat, "And, I'm in a relationship with someone back in Calivada."

I stop and turn to face him, confused. "Did you join the program before you met her?"

He blushes, and looks away, "Actually, no. We have an open relationship. She's with two other men, and I'm allowed to be with other people, too."

Now I'm even more confused, "If you already have someone, though, why would you join the program? It doesn't sound like a marriage is what you're looking for."

He clenches my fingers tightly, "Well, you know I'm an actor. The media got wind of my relationship situation, and they threatened to lock up my girlfriend and her other men if I didn't join. They clearly wanted to make an example of me, given the visibility of the situation."

"Ahh." I say simply. I turn forward and continue walking. He's still holding my hand. "What's her name?"

"Helena," he says softly. "Can you please tell me what you're thinking?"

"I'm not really sure what to think. You don't intend to break it off with her, do you?" I say bluntly.

"No, I don't," he admits, scuffs his boot on one of the stones in the path. "But, you do understand that it's a two-way street for me, right? We'd be married, yes. But you would be able to have a relationship with whoever you wanted, as well. We'd have to live in Calivada, as it's the only place I know of where the government doesn't really have the reach to fully squash it. And most of the women there have at least two children, so you'd be pretty likely to be done at the end of our three-year timeline, if that's what you wanted."

I turn it all over in my mind. What he's suggesting is so far out of left field, I'd never in a million years have thought of it myself. Marry him but still be with whoever I liked. But he'd also be with other women? And how would that feel? Then what, divorce him, come home, and pretend none of it ever happened? I feel troubled, and I'm not sure what to say to him. It sounds like the people of Calivada have found a way to be freer than the rest of us, but I'm not so sure if that's a good thing, or a bad thing.

"I need to think about it for a while, Pierce. Thank you for being honest with me," I finally say. The path we're following has curved back around to the other side of the main hall. He gives my hand a squeeze and lets me go before we walk back in for the announcement.

We find that not only have the women assembled, but all of the remaining bachelors, too, which is unusual. Eric is standing at the front of the room, wearing his signature smile. A guard closes the door after we walk in, and find our way to the back of the group where Matthew, Grant, and Antonio are clustered. Patrick is standing off to the side of the room, and appears to be on duty, but still gives me a brief nod before returning his attention to Eric.

"Good morning everyone! I hope you're all enjoying this time of romance and getting to know your perfect matches!" He looks around, and there is a small rumble of assent from the group. "I'm afraid I have some less-positive news for you all today . . ." He pauses for effect.

"Would it kill him to just say 'bad news' like a normal person?" I hear Beth-Ann whisper-grumble to Phil, who's got his arm around her. He just shakes his head at her.

"The quarterly population reports have been released, and we've reached an all-time low for global population numbers. We have now sunk to the lowest human population in recorded history." He pauses again, and this time the murmurs around the room sound concerned.

"As a result, the NAA government has decided to enact a critical priority measure on the Compulsory Marriage and Reproduction Act."

Jo speaks up, "What does that mean? It's already mandatory —how much more critical can it get?" Her match shifts uncomfortably at her side.

Eric looks around gravely, "There are a few additional measures to be put in place now that the population has reached critical levels. The main one, though, is that there is no longer a release clause once you've had two children. You are still able to separate from your husband if you feel you're incompatible, but you will need to remain in the program."

Jo speaks up again, angrily this time, "For how long? Three kids? What's the number?"

Her match puts a hand on her arm, but she swats him away without a glance.

Eric smiles nervously, "There is no number. The mandate will remain in place until the population as a whole leaves the critical range."

Gasps erupt around the group. Jo's face turns red, and she clenches her fists. I see her match—Elijah, I think?—try to put another calming hand on her, but she's not having it. "I told you to keep your slimy hands to yourself!" she shouts at him, uncaring that everyone is staring at them.

Elijah steps back, a displeased look on his face, "Now be reasonable, Josephine. It's for the greater good."

"I don't give two figs about the greater good! This is basically slavery! You can't keep us in this damn program forever!" She spins angrily and approaches Eric. "I won't do it! There is nothing you can say that will make me marry this little weasel, and I'm certainly not going to waste my life moving from man to man at some program director's whim! It's unconstitutional!" She's shouting, and from the side door I see two burly guards enter. She doesn't see them, though, so caught up in her rage at Eric.

"Josephine, I hope you understand there's nothing any of us can do!" Eric has both hands up, but his placating tone isn't working for her.

"This is BS! Of course there's something you can do—let us live our own friggin' lives!" The guards reach her, and as soon as the first one grabs her arm she takes a swing at him. "Get your hands off of me! I mean it, I will kick you in the balls if you don't back off!"

Instead of releasing her, the second guard grabs her other arm tightly. She makes good on her threat, and knees guard-one in between his legs, he hunches, but doesn't release her. Dr. Mitch appears out of thin air with a syringe in hand.

"Oh, my god, what are they doing to her!" I clutch Matthew's sleeve, and go to run forward. He grabs me around the waist.

Dr. Mitch grabs her head and forces it to the side, plunging the needle into her neck.

"No, Sadie, you don't want to get in the middle of that," Antonio agrees.

"We can't just let them do this to her! Let go of me!" I twist, and manage to escape by ducking under Matthew's arm. Before I've made it three steps out of his reach, Patrick appears in front of me, blocking my way.

He grabs me in a bear hug, pinning my arms to my sides. I struggle, but he leans down close to my ear, "Sadie, I promise you we will help her. But you can't help her if you're sedated with her."

I'm furious, but I stop struggling. He's right, but it eats me up inside to watch the two guards hauling a limp Josephine out of the room between them. Beth-Ann looks like she might faint. Phil is holding her up. Several of the other girls are sobbing and clutching onto their match, or each other. But not me. I can't find tears for this moment, only rage. The door swings shut behind them, and I turn my eyes to Patrick.

"Nothing about this is okay." My voice shakes.

He nods, and loosens his grip a bit, "I agree, Sadie. I agree."
His voice is as solemn as I feel.

FOURTEEN
SHOTGUN WEDDING

As much as I want to go find the gym and punch something for a while, I've got a date and Beth-Ann's wedding this afternoon. I try my best to put on a happy face for my date with Patrick, but it's obvious neither of us is really feeling it after what just went down with Jo. I groom up Hercules, and Patrick chooses Maggie, a beautiful bay mare. Michael does his thing with Patrick and Maggie in the round pen while I let Hercules steal a few illicit bites of the manicured lawn.

They finish up quickly, and we're off. Today we pick a yellow trail marker, and we're instantly plunged into thicker forest than I've seen so far. The chill in the air makes me pull my flannel further down my arms. We ride in silence for several minutes, neither of us wanting to break the calm. Eventually, I decide to ask, "How did you learn to ride so well? Did you have horses growing up?"

"No, actually, but one of my good friends from school did. My parents had to travel often for my father's job, and I'd sometimes stay with his family for two weeks at a time. His mom taught me when I was with them," he says casually.

"Wow, that must have been really hard, being away from your family for so long. How old were you when he started traveling like that?" My interest is pulled off of horsemanship, and onto young Patrick.

He takes a moment before answering, "It could get lonely at times, but Steve's parents made me feel like I belonged. Sometimes it was nice to pretend I was just their other son, you know? That I wouldn't have to go home when my parents came back. I was probably around ten when his traveling went from a few times a year to most of the month."

I can feel my heart pull at his words. "I'm so sorry. Do you and Steve stay in touch?"

"Oh, it's all right," he says lightly. "And we do stay in touch! I spend my holidays from work with them. My dad is still working and traveling most of the time, so they aren't usually home for me to visit."

There's another natural lull in the conversation. Our horses are continuing along, following the trail without much help from us. I let my mind wander. I'm torn between incredibly sad for Patrick that he has so little contact with his family, and incredibly relieved for myself that he'd probably be willing to stay near my own family. Most of my matches are these powerful, well-off men who came from all over the NAA. Of those who are left, only Patrick and Grant actually live in Georada. I shove thoughts of the other men aside, focusing back on Patrick.

"So, Glitch is really something else." I change the subject to something a little more upbeat.

Patrick chuckles, "Yeah, you could say that. He's a good guy."

"How long have you two known each other?" I ask.

"I guess it's been about two years now, since I entered the Guard service. We both started at the same time," he says right as our trail empties into a small clearing.

We guide the horses towards the right side of the clearing, and they happily walk around the edge while stealing snatches of the taller grass. "So, is he tech support for the guards or something?"

"Well, not exactly." Patrick shifts in his saddle, "Technically he's just a regular guard, like me."

Realization dawns on me, "Are you telling me he somehow gave himself access to the security cameras, plus all of that extra Bachelor Book information? He's not supposed to have that?"

"Not so much, no. But please don't mention it to anyone, because we'd all get in pretty big trouble for that. That's just Glitch for you, though. Wherever we work he has to have *access*. He is the most brilliant person I've ever met, and I think that's the only reason he hasn't been caught," he says with a nervous edge.

"I won't say anything. The security cameras make sense, you two being guards and all. But, why hack the Bachelor Book?" That part doesn't make sense to me.

He doesn't answer for a beat, and I look over to see the faintest hint of a blush spreading up his tanned neck.

"Oh my gosh! You put him up to it, didn't you? What, were you checking out the competition or something?" I stifle a laugh at his embarrassment. He's so *cute!*

"Hey, can you blame me? The rumors started spreading about a record-breaking number of matches. I needed the inside scoop to have any shot of matching up against all those hot shots. Plus, it took him like twelve minutes, and he loved it," he justifies.

Now I'm just grinning at him, "So, if you asked him to hack into the Bachelor Book for you, you must have really liked me."

He pretends he didn't hear me, "Hey, look! There's the trail marker again. Do you want to do another lap, or should we head back and get you ready for Phil and Beth-Ann's wedding?"

I sigh, my care-free bubble popped, "Yes, I guess we should go back. Are you coming to the wedding?"

"I'm scheduled to work tonight, unfortunately."

We ride back down the little trail, and banter back and forth along the way. After we unsaddle, we both give our mounts a cool-down brush before saying goodbye. We're standing outside the barn when he reaches over and twines his fingers with mine.

"I'd love to give you another goodbye kiss, but I'm pretty sure you'd rather that news not get around to your other matches," he says, and I appreciate his consideration. "I'm pretty sure the bushes have eyes around here." He glances conspicuously over his shoulder, to where Michael is whistling and polishing a bridle in the doorway.

"Probably for the best," I agree with a chuckle. "So, have you been to a lot of weddings here?" I ask as we start walking slowly back towards the dorms.

"No, not really. I've only been to one before this. The groups are usually a lot smaller than this, and most of them don't ever see us guards, let alone invite us to their big day," he states.

"Is our group really that much different?" I'm surprised to hear that.

"Yes, it really is. There usually aren't ten girls at once, and also the kidnapping attempt was pretty far out there. I've been guarding New Life Centers for two years, and that was only my second one. And the first one was amateur hour by comparison; it was a girl's boyfriend from home who tried to spring her in the middle of the night," he snorts. "It's pretty ridiculous how night and day different that was."

"Aww, he must have really missed her. Poor guy. What happened to him?"

"He got sent home, and she got married the next day. The NLC does *not* take the whole no-illegal-relationships thing lightly."

"Well, it could be worse." *Guess they can't get away with treating men how they treated Josephine.* I keep my morose thoughts to myself as he drops me off by the front steps.

An hour later, I'm showered, dressed, and seated next to Beth-Ann in the bride's room of the dormitory. Elena and Jenna volunteered to be the hair crew, and we're going all out getting dolled up for Beth-Ann. I wouldn't say it's truly a jovial atmosphere, but we're trying for her sake. Jenna has her signature loud, upbeat music pumping through the speaker system.

"It's just so exciting!" Elena says while brandishing a hot curling iron far too close to my face for comfort, "You're the first one of our group to get married! How does it feel? Are you excited? Nervous? Nauseous?"

Jenna giggles, "I'm pretty sure she knows what's going to happen tonight, seeing as they've dated for what, three years, you said?" She looks to Beth-Ann for confirmation.

Beth-Ann smiles happily, "Yes, three years! I knew he was the one from the very beginning." She sighs dreamily, "And no, I'm not nervous about tonight. More so about the permanence of marriage. I love him so much, I just hope it stays this way for life, you know? What if he gets tired of me, or doesn't find me attractive anymore after I have a baby?" she says with a worried frown. "Or what if my parents drive him off?"

"Beth-Ann, you're going to be married. Even if they try to split you two up, it will be up to you and Phil to decide to stay together," I say in my best "keep calm" voice.

"Yeah, and surely they'll get on board once you have a grandbaby to spoil. Aren't they in politics? Carrying on the family line looks *particularly good* in re-election campaigns, and a messy divorce could really blow up their perfect image. Just work that angle," Jenna says confidently.

"You really think having a family matters in the elections? Being childless has no bearing on your ability to do the job at hand," I argue.

"No, she's right," Beth-Ann agrees. "It's been a few years, but I remember my dad saying a vote had been put up about switching the NAA to a monarchy, since voting has been getting harder to maintain as cities keep getting closed and citizens moved all over the country. It didn't pass at the time, but he said it's come up twice already. My dad says people trust politicians with families more than those without." She stops talking abruptly when Jenna starts coating her hair in a toxic cloud of hairspray, while dancing back and forth to the song that just came on.

"Good lordy, I think that's enough," I cough out. "My eyelashes are going to get stuck together just being next to you."

Jenna stops spraying, but switches to some dance with aggressive fist pumping and jogging to the beat. "Don't worry, your turn with the can is coming," she finally says when she stops.

Elena pipes up, "But, how could they switch us to a monarchy when there's no ruling family? I mean, who would be the king and queen? Do they already have kids?" The curling iron veers so close to my neck I can feel the heat through the bottom layer of my hair. I flinch to the side and she snatches it back, pulling my roots.

Beth-Ann thinks for a minute before responding, "Well, they'd probably appoint someone who's already high up in government.. Prime Minister Royce has two kids, but nobody knows much about them. I think he's pretty popular, too. He's been re-elected for most of the last ten years, maybe more — they might just elect him." She shifts in her seat, and Jenna freezes with bobby pins in her mouth.

"Holf stiwwl owr Ihm goihnn to pohkh you," Jenna grumbles.

"What?" Beth-Ann asks, shifting again.

"HOLF SWIWWL OWR IHM GOIGNN TO POKHHH YUHHH!" she mumbles louder.

"Hold still or she's going to poke you with a bobby pin," Elena translates.

"Oh, sorry!" Beth-Ann looks sheepish.

"I still just can't imagine the NAA as a monarchy," I say, still caught up on the whole politics discussion, "I know the re-election limits were dropped when my parents were kids, because the political pool is too small to change leadership so often. But, I mean, that's a huge change for the country." I lean forward, getting into the conversation.

Elena flicks me on the forehead, "Now you hold still or you're going to get your neck burnt!"

Beth-Ann laughs, "You two are dictators! You're not the Royces, you can't tell us what to do!" she jokes.

Jenna slides the last pin into Beth-Ann's hair, and then gestures animatedly with a round brush, "It's not like they're opposed to changing things, especially after that announcement this morning. I read through some more of the details of the official announcement, and the only way to get out of being pushed from man to man is after three failed matches, you can switch to using a sperm donor, but only if you have family or husband who isn't a genetic match willing to take you in and sign an agreement to help care for the children."

"That's outrageous!" Elena says, "So what happens if you are successful with the sperm donor? How many kids do you have to have?"

"That part's even worse," she says angrily, "You have to report to your nearest NLC and stay until you're successfully pregnant, however long that takes. Then, even after you give birth you only have eighteen months after until you have to report back again and repeat the process."

"Okay, so two more kids? I mean it sucks but that's not as bad as it could be." Beth-Ann tries to reason it out.

"Oh, you didn't let me finish. You have to keep coming back until one of the NLC doctors will declare you menopausal or otherwise physically unable to get pregnant. So, some women that's until their late forties." We all go quiet after she drops that bomb.

My mind is reeling. My parents have seven kids. I'm some sort of fertility wonder, and birth control is illegal. I quickly run through the math and realize that even if I'm only fertile until I'm forty-five, I could end up with nearly a dozen kids. "Holy crap on a cracker. What if you can't handle that many kids? What are you supposed to do? Most people don't have families big enough to help take care of that many!" I say, feeling panicked. "There *has* to be a limit."

Jenna shakes her head, and picks up another stack of bobby pins, "You can read the announcement tonight, they sent it to all of our tablets. But I didn't see anything about a limit."

Nell and Leigh walk in, holding makeup cases.

"Aren't you two done yet? We need to switch and get started on make-up!" Leigh says in a sing-song voice. "Who wants to let me do their face?" she waggles the case excitedly.

"Bride first!" Jenna orders, and Leigh pops open both cases next to Beth-Ann.

"Just you wait, Beth-Ann—Phil isn't even going to recognize you when we're done with you!" Leigh starts slathering various color options onto her wrist.

Nell snorts, "Don't we want him to recognize her? They actually like each other. Wouldn't that be nice," she mutters the last bit under her breath.

"Still not a big fan of Atlas, huh? Even with all those muscles? If Hector wasn't so dreamy, I'd totally trade you. I bet he could pick you up with one arm. You should ask him!" Elena says.

"He's fine, I guess. But I am definitely not asking him to pick me up with one arm," Nell protests. "Plus, trading would defeat the purpose of this whole system."

The girls continue their happy banter, but it washes over me, lost as I am in my panic over the possibility of having twelve or more children. There's just no way. I can't be pregnant that long, I can't give birth that many times, and I certainly can't not work for that long. My family are ranchers, for Pete's sake. That's a lot of physical labor that I just couldn't do pregnant or while chasing an endless stream of toddlers. I have to find a way out—there's no other choice.

Elena taps me on the shoulder, "Sadie, did you hear me? You're done. Go grab your dress!"

"Oh, sorry, Elena. Thank you, it looks great, really," I say absently before leaving the room to retrieve my dress.

The Georada New Life Center apparently has a full outdoor wedding venue. Beth-Ann and I are waiting just inside the sports center, getting ready to walk over. She chose a tea length cream gown, with a blush satin ribbon around the waist. She has a small bouquet of purple flowers in one hand, and is tapping idly with the other against the door handle. Once you choose to get married here, they have a wedding planning team to quickly implement the details for you. It's really interesting to see how they've managed it. She filled out a survey with her dress size, favorite colors, which on-site venue she preferred, and a few other preferences. A dress rack was delivered to her room that night, and her bouquet to the bride's room thirty minutes ago with instructions to wait here for our escort to the venue. I offered to wait with her, but everyone else will already be there when we arrive.

"Surely it's bad luck to make the bride stand around and wait before the wedding," Beth-Ann grumbles. "I'm starving, and nauseous, and second guessing my gown choice." She gives the door handle a loud thump.

"They should be here any minute. Do you want one of these crackers?" I pull them out of my pocket where I'd stashed them earlier, but she waves me off and spins to face the sports center.

"This place is pretty cool. It's a shame we haven't had a chance to use it yet. Although Phil told me a lot of the guys hang out in here between dates. They've got courts for almost everything including some virtual stuff, and then two separate mini-theaters for watching sports when there's a live game." Her rambling is cut off by the door clicking open. A prim-looking woman who appears to be in her sixties pokes her head in.

"Beth-Ann? I'm Melinda. Are you ready to head to the wedding?" she asks politely.

"Finally! Yes, let's get this show on the road, because I'm starving." She blows past Melinda, who looks at me, mildly shocked.

"Well, I must say, I've never had that response from the bride before and I've been at this for some time!" She pats her sprayed-stiff hair before turning and following Beth-Ann.

I chuckle and follow them out. A short walk across the perfectly manicured lawns, and we arrive at an outdoor theater. It's built into one of the natural hills, and it's quite pretty. There is a permanent archway at the front with trailing vines growing over it, and lightly wrapped with tulle. Underneath it stands none other than Eric with a nervous-looking Phil. His face lights up when he sees Beth-Ann.

Melinda pulls a mini-tablet out of her dress pocket, and taps a few buttons which cue up the bridal march. Beth-Ann didn't even wait for me to take a seat first, so I just sit down in the back row after she marches herself to where Phil is waiting. The other girls are all here, and all dressed in various shades of purple, like me. A few of them have dates along, but most of us don't. I wanted to focus on Beth-Ann since she told me they'll be leaving tonight after the ceremony and dinner.

"Welcome, friends! We are here today to celebrate the union of Beth-Ann and Phil on the most important day of their lives. I am so honored to have been able to participate in my own small way in bringing you two to this most happy of moments!"

God, he's obnoxious. They were already together before this whole farce! My mind starts to wander, but he quickly gets to the vows.

"If you'd repeat after me—'I, Beth-Ann, do take you, Phil,'" he says, solemn.

"I, Beth-Ann, do take you, Phil," she repeats.

"Is this seat taken?" A masculine voice speaks next to my ear, and I nearly jump out of my skin.

"Good Lord!" I whisper-shout and clutch my chest.

Eric clears his throat loudly at the front, and I see that everyone has turned to stare at my outburst.

"Sorry! Sorry, carry on!" I say with embarrassment and grab Patrick's wrist, dragging him into the seat next to me.

Eric scolds us with his eyes as he says the next line, but I ignore him. Whispering, I lean closer to Patrick, "What are you doing here? I thought you were on duty this afternoon?"

"Glitch swapped with me so I could surprise you. He got caught up in the middle of one of his projects, though, which is why I'm a little late. Sorry," he whispers back.

I nod and try to focus back in on the ceremony. It is over in minutes, and Eric announces the happy couple who then lead the way towards the main dining hall for the celebratory dinner. Beth-Ann wiggles her bouquet in the air the whole way. We stay seated and let most of the group head out ahead of us. Eric approaches Margaret and offers his arm, but she says something to him under her breath before walking off ahead of him. He trails behind her, but not before looking around to see if anyone noticed. I quickly look to Patrick, who looks down at his feet.

After Eric passes us, we get up and follow everyone to the reception.

While I should be happy for my friend getting to marry someone she actually loves, all I feel inside is hollow. The memory of Josephine being sedated and dragged away by armed guards this morning is burned into the backs of my eyelids. But as much as I want to let out my rage, I force myself to lock it inside. *Because I don't want to be next.*

Fifteen
RIPPLE EFFECT

D ays pass, following the same familiar rhythm. Dates are scheduled, activities shared, and meals eaten over forced polite conversation. The rest of the week passes without further event. At the end, a pale and queasy Charlotte returns from her procedure with two smitten men in tow. A small part of me is glad to see that Devonte is one of them, while the rest of me is just numb.

Another week passes, then two. Teddy has checked on me twice, but I don't know what to tell him. My head and my heart are both jumbled up. I continue on with the motions of the program, and am unsurprised to see our numbers begin to dwindle. Leigh releases Spencer after a long-overdue conversation with Faith, and we all watch from the veranda as he shouts at the driver before boarding the shuttle.

But still, Josephine never returns to us.

I have a few solo dates with one of the guys each day, and tonight I'm scheduled to go out with Matthew. He didn't tell me what we would be doing, just to meet him on the porch and dress comfortably. I head down the stairs, and as soon as I open the door I see him standing there, with a wrapped box in his hands.

"Hey Matt!"

"Hey beautiful," he crosses the distance between us, and kisses me on the cheek. "This is for you," he states simply and hands me the box.

I smile at his thoughtfulness. "You didn't have to get me anything!"

"It's for our date. Go on, open it." He sounds excited, which makes me more excited to see what's in the box. However, when I open it, I'm confused.

"Uhm, who's Steinboldt?" I ask, as I hold up a large blue and white jersey with the name printed on the back.

He grins, "Come on, I'll show you." He takes my hand, and we walk to the sports complex.

We walk down the hall to one of the theaters, which has a "Reserved" sign on the front. He holds open the door for me, and I can see he has put a lot of effort into this date.

There are plush theater seats filling the room, and to the side there is a table laden with popcorn, hotdogs, sodas, and every other food you can imagine at a sporting event.

"Do I smell funnel cake?" I ask, excited at the possibility of my favorite junk food.

"You do. A little birdie told me it was your favorite. I thought this evening, we could share some of our favorites. I am a die-hard ice hockey fan, and I made sure to have the kitchen make up every one of your favorite treats."

I'm touched by his thoughtful gestures, and after loading up plates full of junk food, we take the two prime seats in the middle of the room.

The room darkens seemingly of its own accord, and the screen fills with a rink, with players skating out from either end.

"So, are we rooting for the blue guys?" I guess, based on the color of my jersey.

He chuckles, "Yes, the blue guys. We're going to send the orange guys home in a body bag. Look! There's Steinboldt!" Matt's enthusiasm is infectious, and I thoroughly enjoy watching him get riled up about his favorite sport. He spends the evening telling me all the rules, most of which I can't remember. *But, if I choose him, we could have a lifetime to do this on Saturday nights.*

When the game ends, he flops back against his seat and looks over at me, a satisfied grin plastered across his handsome face. For the first time ever, I feel like he's let me see him as a regular guy, not just a businessman.

"I like you," I say.

His eyebrows come down, "Uhm, I like you, too . . ." he says, unsure of where the conversation is going.

"As a person, I mean. Yes, you're Mr. Powerful Businessman. But tonight, I feel like I finally got to know *Matt*. And I like him." I look down, feeling shy at the admission.

"Hey," he waits until I meet his eyes again, "Thank you for saying that. Not many people can see that there's more to me than money and a job. Everyone I meet just wants to pitch me their business idea." He snorts. "And most of them are utter crap, at that."

I sit bolt upright, "Oh! I know this is horrible timing. But, I actually did have a business idea!"

He laughs so hard at that, he turns red. "Are you serious right now? You are crazy. In the best kind of way." He leans forward, and before I even realize what's happening, he smacks a kiss right on my lips. "Tell me your business idea. Is it horse related?"

My brain is still back on the sudden kiss, but I force it to focus, "Uh, well, do you know anything about candle making?

Because I think you could sell a bunch that smell like leather. Or fresh hay. It's probably the best smell in the world."

He shakes his head, "Sorry, I know less than nothing about candles. I don't think I even own a candle. But you could start your own candle business, if you want." He taps me on the nose.

"I figured. But hey, you never know unless you ask."

Later that night, I've just settled in with the girls to watch a movie in the sitting area when my mini-tablet buzzes. I see a request from Patrick—for right now. *That's odd, I'm scheduled to see him tomorrow.* I accept, and then slip on my shoes and head out the front door, only to find nobody there.

Frowning, I look around and still don't see anything. Then, I hear music coming from the side of the house. I walk around, and there he is, with a single rose. "Patrick, what are you doing out here? And where's the music coming from?"

He smiles, and hands me the rose, "It's a secret. I got off my shift, and the night was so beautiful and clear, that I had to see if I could steal a little of your time. Would you dance with me, Sadie?" He threads his fingers through mine, and he sways invitingly.

"Out here?"

He leans in close before answering, "Right here, right now."

The words send a shiver through me, and I nod in acceptance. He plucks the rose from my fingertips, and sets it in the grass before pulling me into a slow, smooth dance. The cool air and gorgeous moon are our only companions in this little slice of heaven on earth.

I could stay like this forever.

After four or five songs, he hugs me tightly to his chest. "Thank you for spending some time with me, Sadie. I know we have a date tomorrow, but I couldn't wait another minute to see you again." His look is intense, and I find myself gravitating even closer to him.

He leans in, and when our lips meet, it feels like the electricity should light up the night. When he pulls back again, I let out a gentle sigh.

"I think you might be too perfect," I say. "I didn't think they made men like you in the real world."

He grins, but instead of responding, just kisses me again. Heat blossoms all the way to my toes.

"Oh yeah, getting some sugar!" I hear Jenna's voice from the porch railing, and spring back from Patrick, hand to my lips.

"Oh my word, would you go back inside!" I yell as I turn, and spot not just Jenna, but all the girls lined up and spying on us.

When I turn back around, Patrick is trying his hardest not to laugh. "We can call it a night. Thank you, Sadie." With one last peck on the cheek, he leaves me to merciless girls singing infantile kissing songs on the porch. *Nuts, every one of them.*

Another week passes, and we're all brought in to the clinic for another round of fertility testing, so the medical team can compare our results with our tracker's first month of data. It's invasive, and they take more blood. I stare out the window and pretend that I'm anywhere else. I dream at night of riding Morgan through a pasture dotted with wildflowers, laughing with one of my brothers as we check fences.

One morning, I'm awoken by a knock, instead of the usual windchimes. It takes me a moment to realize what's happening, but I quickly stumble out of bed and to the door. I pull it open expecting one of the other girls, but instead see Teddy.

"May I come in, or are you going to bite me? You've got that haven't-been-caffeinated-yet look going on," he jokes.

I step to the side while rubbing one bleary eye with the heel of my hand, "Get in here and give me a minute. I wasn't awake yet."

He steps inside, and I shut the door. I point to the bench by my bed, and hustle into the bathroom to quickly pee and brush my teeth. Once I'm a little more presentable and mostly awake, I sit down in the desk chair across from him. He's made himself at home, and brewed coffee in my previously unused coffee maker.

"Ugh, that stuff is stinking up the place," I complain.

He chuckles, "Yeah, yeah. Don't knock it until you try it." He takes another sip and gives me a devilish grin.

"So, to what do I owe the displeasure of your early-morning mug?" I ask, poking at his knee with my foot.

"Well, I think it's time we had a conversation. Faith got her secondary fertility results yesterday, and doctor douchebag told her that as early as next week she'll be ready for, uh . . ." he pauses, unsure how to continue.

I just stare at him, refusing to make this easy. You barge into my room and wake me before the butt crack of dawn, you get to roll around in your own awkwardness while I stare you down.

After a second when he realizes I'm really not coming to his rescue he says, "She'll be ready for planting?" then winces.

"Eww, really? Can't you just say baby-making like a normal person? What are you, five?" I can't think about any of my brothers *planting* anybody. Blech. Gag me.

"Moving on!" He averts his gaze. "Faith asked me if I'd be willing to move the wedding up and go ahead and get this show on the road. I get where she's coming from, and I don't want to drag this out for her any more than the past six years already have." He stops, and looks at me to gauge my reaction.

"Okay, and . . .?" I prompt.

"Well, the whole reason I came here is to be here for you, and make sure you're okay. You still haven't picked yet, and frankly you don't seem any closer to narrowing it down. It's been a month, and you still have five matches waiting for your decision. I don't feel like I can leave and do this with Faith, with you no closer to a real match. What's going on, Sadie?"

It's my turn to look away. I've been so up in my own head recently, and so mad about Josephine, that I haven't even tried to whittle down my matches further. I sigh, "You're right. I should probably let some of them go today."

"Look, I am not here worried about those dudes. They're grown, and they'll live with whatever you decide. You're my baby sister. I want to know why you've been checked out. You're not you lately, Sadie. What can I do to fix it?" He leans forward and rests his hands on both of my knees. "Talk to me, or I'm not leaving."

I rest my hands on top of his larger ones, "I don't even know, myself," I confess. "I am just so torn up inside and mad about what they did to Josephine. They won't tell me where she is, do you know that? It's been weeks, and nothing. Did they ship her off? Her match disappeared, too. Did they kick her out? Was she penalized? Nothing, nada, zip. I have beaten on every door in this place, and Patrick has asked everyone above him in the guard, and nobody knows where she is, or at least they're not saying." I swallow, but the lump in my throat won't budge.

"I just hate this, Teddy. Nobody should be able to have this much power over another human. Does her family even know she's gone, or if she's gone? What if they've locked her in like, NLC jail until she promises to behave? She never will! And what's to say I won't be next, Teddy? If you weren't here, I would just be gone, and nobody at home would ever know what they did to me. It's not right!" My voice cracks. "Remember Aisha, who was a few years older than me?"

"Yeah, what about her?"

"Well, she enrolled in the program late, like I did. Didn't want to go, left behind her high school sweetheart. And she just never came back. Her parents got a letter in the mail a year later that she'd died in childbirth, delivering a baby boy. They spent months trying to get the baby, but eventually they got another rejection letter, stating that the baby had already been adopted through some orphan program, for couples who are completely sterile. That's it, she was just gone, and all her parents got was a letter. They didn't even get a body to bury! Nothing!" I hide my face in my hands.

His arms come up, and he wraps me in a hug, "Shh, sister, it's all going to be okay." I try to protest, but he cuts me off, "I'm not saying it's right. It's not right, not at all. But you aren't alone. You have me, and I'm not going to let anything happen to you. Plus, you have all these matches trying to plant you, I don't think they'll be letting you out of their sight. Especially that Matthew guy, he's intense."

I shove him back, "Ok, you dope, enough with the planting. It's a gross metaphor." I scrub at a tear that dared escape.

He reaches over and ruffles my bedhead. "You're not going to die in childbirth; Mom delivered seven of us just fine, so you've got rock star genes. You saw what happened to Josephine, and I know you'd never make a scene like that and get in trouble." He raises both hands, "I'm not justifying it, just saying it won't happen to you."

I glare at him anyways. "Speaking of rock star genes, I'm not the only one." I forgot to tell him about his likely genetic unicorn status.

"Ehh, I'm just a man—nobody cares about my awesome genes." He brushes me off.

"No, Teddy, I'm serious. I haven't had a minute alone with you to tell you before now," I urge, not wanting him to take this lightly. "I found out that the NLC scientists think our family has some sort of—what did they call it?—polymorphic gene, which means we're no longer affected by the Sterilization Vector. I'm normal, and you probably are, too."

He leans back on the bench, serious again. "How did you find that out?"

"Patrick's friend, Glitch. I think he's some sort of hacker, and he had access to all this information about everyone. They think the kidnapping attempt when we first got here might have been directed at me," I admit.

My usually jovial brother's face darkens immediately, "Are you trying to tell me they let people who were trying to kidnap you —not just one of the women, but YOU, specifically—get that close?" He stands up and starts to pace. "There's no way I can leave with Faith, then. Not until you're ready to go with us. What if they come back? I would never forgive myself if you got snatched when I was on some beach somewhere sipping piña coladas."

"They haven't come back, so clearly they've given up. I am not going to stop you and Faith from getting this over with and getting out of this program."

"Sadie, did you not hear the announcement last month? There is no 'getting out' anymore, for you or Faith. We're all officially in this for the long haul," he states, momentarily stopping his pacing.

"Yeah, sure, I did hear that. Trust me, I haven't forgotten. But you're a man! You see out your time with Faith, and you two can part ways as friends, and you can go live your normal life. I'm apparently fertile, so I shouldn't have to go back into the matching program so long as my husband doesn't completely suck."

He's staring at me, "You think that just because I'm a man and *can* divorce Faith when this is over, that that's what I'll do? Did you not grow up in the same house I did, with Mom and Dad spouting constantly about how marriage is for life? All the rest of these people might feel like marriage is something to slap on and off like a wet raincoat, but you and I both know better. No, once I'm in, I'm in for life." He points a finger at me, as if punctuating the sentiment.

I frown, "Have you spoken to Faith about how you feel about marriage?"

He waves a hand up and down, dismissing my question, "Don't try to change the subject—I already know they've made her divorce twice. She gets a pass; she didn't have an option either time."

"No, that's not what I mean—" I start again, but he cuts me off.

"But, hey—upside to you being a poly-whatcha-ma-call-it— I've probably got some super sperm and we shouldn't have much trouble having a baby. Did you hear we're actually a ninety-nine percent match? Cool, huh?" He seems cheerful, practically chipper. He's now moving stuff around on my desk, looking for something to fidget with. He finds a rubber-band ball and starts tossing it.

"Teddy, will you shut up for a minute? I'm serious." I use my sternest voice.

"What?" He keeps tossing the ball, but he shuts up at least.

"Have you asked Faith how she feels about staying married? Does she also want to be married, happily ever after, and the whole 'forever' shebang with you? Because that's not the impression I got from her before." I pause, not wanting to burst his bubble, but also feeling the need to protect him. "She told *me* that she wants to go back to New Texas. That once she's had the required number of kids, she wants to take the kids and live on her own, in her family home."

Teddy's next catch misses, and the rubber-band ball goes rolling off under my unmade bed. "She said that? When?"

"Well, it was before you got here. But she is tired of being jerked around all over and seemed pretty set on it. You should probably let her in on the whole literal interpretation of 'till death do us part' before you run off and marry her early." To my utter shock, he seems to deflate at my words.

"I can't believe she feels that way." He sits back on the bench at the foot of the bed, looking shocked.

"Really? You really can't understand it? Because I can, and this is my first time getting matched. She's already been through this twice, Teddy. And from the sounds of it, her second match was a real piece of work," I say, softer now. I sit next to him, and this time it's me putting an arm around his shoulders for comfort.

He snorts angrily, "Yeah—Spencer? Total douche-nozzle. I'd love an hour alone with that guy and my police baton."

I smack his arm, "Best to just let that go, don't you think? He's out of her life now."

We sit quietly for a few minutes, and then, the sound of my usual morning windchimes start echoing through my room. Teddy makes his exit, and I get ready for the day. I've got some men to send home today. The only question is, which ones?

SIXTEEN
LETTING GO

I scheduled dates with all five of my remaining matches today, and it's going to be the last day here for a few of them. Maybe four of them, I haven't decided. It's time to hammer out some details. I fidget with the hem of my favorite green flannel shirt, dreading my first date. I've been getting to know each of these men, so I feel like I owe it to each of them to let them know in person if I'll be releasing them, and say goodbye. It seems cold to do it any other way at this point, but I still dread letting them down. Surprisingly enough, each man pulls out a different part of my personality, and I do feel a connection with each of them on some level, but it's time.

I'm waiting on the dormitory porch, staring out over the rolling green lawns when Pierce walks up and greets me, "Good morning, Sadie. You look lovely as always," he says smoothly.

"Hey Pierce," I say, locking eyes with him, "I was hoping you wouldn't mind having a talk with me. Care to swing a bit?" I gesture towards the swings at either end of the porch.

He ascends the stairs and slips his hand around my waist. We walk together towards the swing on the right side of the porch, so we're looking back down the long curving driveway. We sit quietly for a moment, and I get us swinging just so. He rests one palm on my thigh and gives me a small squeeze.

"So, it's time, isn't it?" he surprises me by asking.

I'm staring at my feet, unable to look at him now. "Yes, I think it is."

He reaches up and swipes a strand of hair behind my ear. "I'm pretty sure I know why, but, can we talk about it anyways?" he asks quietly.

I take a deep breath, "Of course. You're a really great guy, and at risk of stating the obvious, extremely handsome. Any girl would be lucky to catch you and make little movie-star babies with you," I begin. "But the thing is, Helena has already caught you. And as much as I respect you as a person, I don't think that the lifestyle you want is the one that's right for me. I want you to know, I did consider it. I didn't keep you here for nothing —the idea of a small amount of freedom is hard to resist, and you're so charming. But when it comes down to it . . . that's not who I am."

He's looking off into the distance when he responds a moment later, "That's what I assumed, but I appreciate you telling me. For what it's worth, you're a really great girl. One of these men is extremely lucky that you're going to choose him, don't forget that, okay? Just because they want to act like you have no options, and only one value, doesn't mean it's true. You have the potential to do and be so much more, Sadie, if you just open yourself to it. If it wasn't for Helena, I could see you and I making a memorable life together."

I'm floored, but the words mean a lot to me, and I tuck them away to pull out and examine another time. "Thank you, Pierce, that really means a lot."

He gives me a weak smile, "All right then, I guess I'll go start packing." With one last kiss on the cheek, he walks back to the men's dormitory and out of my life.

My next date is with Grant, who I choose to meet at the stables as is our custom. I'm a few minutes early since my talk with Pierce didn't take long, so I make the rounds and give each horse a biscuit, before getting to work grooming and saddling Hercules.

"You really are a pretty fella, Herckie-Herc. I wish you and I could just ride off into the sunset together, we'd have a blast. I even have a friend for you back home named Morgan. I bet you two would be thick as thieves in no time, once you sorted out who's boss. What do you say, Herckie? Want to run away with me?" I run the finishing brush up over his hips, and his coat shines like liquid silver. "You're just going to leave a girl hanging even after a proposal like that? And here I thought we were good friends." I give him a scratch behind the ear, and he snorts in response. Man of few words, this one.

I spin to get his saddle where I'd set it on the rack outside the stall door, only to see a grinning Grant leaned against it.

"Speaking of leaving people hanging, you're just going to ride off into the wilds with old Hercules here, and leave us all high and dry, huh?"

"Hey, poke fun if you must, but have you seen this boy? His dapple gray coat would make any female swoon." I give him my best fainting belle impression. "Pass me his blanket?"

He shakes his head at my antics before passing me Hercules's tack. I quickly saddle up, and then he grabs Bullet's reins from the ever-present Michael.

"Which way do you want to go today?" he asks once we're in the courtyard.

"Let's go blue. First one to dismount at the pond wins!" I shout, kicking Hercules into an instant gallop towards the trailhead. He takes off so quickly he flings up clods of dirt from the courtyard.

"Giddup, Bullet!" Grant shouts from behind us, and I can hear his reins slap against Bullet's flank as he urges him to catch us.

The wind whips against my face, and the cool fall air fills my lungs as we race along the winding trail towards the pond. I can hear Bullet closing in behind us and another slap of Grant's reins urging him on. I raise slightly off the saddle, and lean forward towards Hercules's neck, ignoring the small stings of his mane whipping against my face. I kiss to him, and his ears flick back in response. "Come on Herc, let's show those boys what we're made of!" I drop my reins hand down low, giving him his lead. Somehow, he finds another gear and we shoot forward even faster. "That's it, Hercules! We're flying now!" I encourage him, his ears flattening against his head as he flies over the soft trail.

We fly over the soft pine needle ground, and Bullet never catches us. The opening to the pond clearing is suddenly upon us, and without hesitation Hercules charges ahead straight towards the pond. At the last possible moment I sit deeply in the saddle and lean back with a shout, "Ho, Hercules!" He slides to a stop any cutting horse would be proud of as I leap off over his left shoulder. Spinning, I can't help the grin covering my face as I spot Grant and Bullet a full two paces behind us. They never stood a chance. I feel so alive, so giddy in that moment that I feel like Hercules has given me wings. Grant pulls Bullet up a few feet away from me and swings his leg over to step off. He gives him a quick pat on the neck before dropping his reins and closing the distance between us.

"How in tarnation did you get that horse to run so fast? We were gaining on you, and he took off like a rocket. Poor Bullet here didn't stand a chance, and he's a hand taller than Hercules. What's your secret?" he asks conspiratorially.

I laugh letting the lighthearted moment bubble over. I lean in close, and he stiffens just slightly as my breath touches his ear, "I know how to sweet talk the fellas, and that's all you need to know." I punch him lightly on the shoulder and lean back.

"Fine, I see how it is," he says teasing me, "Now, what is it you win exactly, for showing me and poor Bullet up so thoroughly?"

I exaggeratedly tap my chin as I lead Hercules over to the hitching post and tie him up. "How about a game. Truth or dare. But I'll be nice, and let the loser go first, since you clearly need a head start." I gesture to the bench under the closest tree, and we walk over to take a seat in the shade.

"Truth or dare? You know I'm thirty two, not twelve, right?" he says lightly.

I just elbow him in the ribs, and wait for him to ask the question.

He sighs as if I'm torturing him, "All right, what's it going to be? Truth, or dare?"

"Truth." My go-to response. Call me chicken, but girls can get vicious at sleepovers, and old habits die hard.

"Truth, okay. Have you picked someone? Is that why you've asked all of us on dates today, so you can let everyone down easy?"

I'm surprised by his perception, but I shouldn't be. He didn't save his whole town and family business by being obtuse. "Not in so many words, but I think it's time to narrow things down. I need to know at this point if you are, or are not, a contender."

"Fair enough. How far are you planning to narrow things down?" he asks.

"Uh-uh, my turn. Only one question per round. Truth or dare?" I posit.

He looks to the sky, leaning back against the bench for a second before answering. "Truth for truth. What do you want to know?"

I think for a moment, unsure how to best phrase my question without offending him. "Do you find me attractive?" I finally settle on that, as it puts more of the burden on me.

He looks startled, "What? Of course! You're a very attractive woman."

"Okay," I say simply. "Your turn again. I choose truth."

"Well I'm not really sure how to follow that one up. Maybe tit-for-tat. Do you find me attractive?" He looks at me expectantly.

I take my time, and peruse him from his tan cowboy hat, past rugged reddish scruff, down his farm-boy muscles, all the way to the tips of his pointed boots before meeting his eyes again. "Yes, I do." I give him a cheeky smile. "My turn. Truth or dare?"

He clutches his hand to his heart playfully, "I'm not sure I can handle any more truth."

"Okay, then I dare you to kiss me." I say it quickly, before he has a chance to change his mind. I watch intently as his expression changes from playfulness, through surprise, and then to reserve.

"Wait, hold on a minute. Is this some sort of test? Why would you want our first kiss to be here, like this? Physical intimacy is not a game to me, Sadie." He leans away from me. The motion is slight enough I'm not sure he even realizes he's done it, but his discomfort is crystal clear to me.

"Okay, it's fine. We can stop playing. But I still want you to kiss me. Do you even want to kiss me, Grant?" I lean over, and place a hand gently on his forearm, and his flinch is more noticeable this time.

He stares at his boots, and the moment drags on. I already know the answer before he forces himself to look at me again. I move my hand to his shoulder and give it a small reassuring squeeze.

"It's okay if the answer is no, Grant. It really is. I just needed to know that. I'm sorry for pushing you," I say softly.

He sighs, then leans forward and puts his head in his hands, taking off his hat and resting it on one knee in the process. "It's not you, Sadie, it's me." It comes out muffled due to his position.

"Grant, you don't owe me any explanation you don't want to give. We can part as friends." I let my hand fall back to my lap, and look out over the shimmering surface of the pond. I can wait as long as he needs.

Eventually he sits up, and runs his hand roughly through his auburn hair a few times before settling his hat back in place. He turns so he's facing me on the bench, and reaches out to hold one of my hands with both of his. "I meant what I said before, you are a very attractive woman. It's just . . . you're not attractive to me, because I'm not attracted to women." His voice is quiet at the end, as if the confession spoken above a whisper would be too much.

"I kind of guessed, Grant, but I needed to know for sure. I'm not mad. I am curious why you joined this program, though. I mean, only if you want to talk about it." I don't want to pry, but I *am* confused.

He looks down at our hands as it spills out, "I want a son. I want someone to pass on my family's farm to, and there's only one way to do that now. I applied for the orphan adoption program, but they won't even consider you unless you've already been through the matching program and either weren't able to be matched, were found sterile, or were booted."

"That doesn't seem fair. Although, I guess none of this is, really."

We're both silent for a beat.

"If I release you, would this qualify you to re-apply to the adoption program, or will you have to continue meeting matches?" I ask.

"I've been in the program almost four and a half years, and you're the first match they've ever found for me. I'm six months away from being eligible to apply for the adoption program," he says bitterly.

"Well then, that's what you'll have to do." I give him a friendly smile, "I think you'd be a great dad, Grant. I really do."

He gives me a thin smile in return, "Thanks, Sadie. But, how did you know? No one has ever guessed before you."

"Well, to be fair, I had six men to compare you to. You're the only one who hasn't tried to feel me up at least once, or sneak a kiss at least on the cheek. At first I assumed you were just being a true southern gentleman, but over time I suspected there was more to it."

He nods once, then looks over his shoulder at where the horses are waiting. "You ready to ride back? I think Bullet wants a rematch." This time his smile is sincere.

"Oh, Bullet can have as many rematches as he wants, but it won't change a thing!" I spring from the bench, and we both quickly mount back up for the ride home.

We race back to the barn along the serene path, and of course I win again. We walk the horses around a few laps in the courtyard to cool off before bringing them back to their stalls and untacking them. I'm giving Hercules a final pat and a cookie when Grant rejoins me, finished with Bullet.

"Can I walk you back to your place?" he asks.

"Sure, let's go."

We walk in silence, and he escorts me all the way to the porch steps. The silence is companionable, and I think I sense some relief from him that this is over. We stop, and turn to face each other.

"You're nothing like what I expected, in the best possible ways," he says, and I sense that he means it.

"What, you didn't expect to get matched with another ranch hand who could whoop you in a horse race?" I quip.

He grins, "That too, Sadie, that too. If you're ever down my way, will you stop in for a visit? I'd love to show you around my place."

"I'd love that, Grant. I'll try to come by whenever this program finally spits me out."

With that, he tips his hat, and turns and walks back to the men's dorm. I take a deep breath, and then head up to grab my mini-tablet to let him go, too. Two matches down, three to go.

Lunchtime rolls around, and it's time to meet Antonio. I change into fresh jeans and a new flannel, pink this time, before heading over to the dining hall. Antonio is waiting for me in the entryway, chatting with a bored guard. He's holding a small bouquet of red roses.

"Hey Antonio." I walk up, and he immediately shifts his attention to me.

"Sadie! You look beautiful as ever!" He grabs me by the shoulders and air kisses both cheeks.

"Thank you. Are those for me?" I point to the bouquet.

He smacks his forehead before handing them over, "Yes, of course! I hope you like red?"

"They're lovely, thank you for thinking of me," I say sincerely, looking down at them. *Passionate love*—that's what my mother would say about this bouquet. I shift to my other foot, uncomfortable.

"Is everything all right, dear?" he asks, more softly this time.

I snap my head up, looking back at him, "Yes, of course. They just made me think of my mother, that's all. She's the gardener of our family, and grows flowers to share with her friends at church." The smile I give him is thin, and there's not a thing I can do about it.

"Ahh, missing home? I can't say I blame you, I'm missing my daughter as well." He shoves his hands into his slacks pockets, "Shall we get started on our date? What are we doing, by the way? All it said was 'lunch activity.'"

"Oh! Uhm, well, I hope you don't mind, but on our last date, you told us about how your grandmother made amazing pasta. So, I contacted the kitchen staff and asked if we could have the supplies and space in the kitchen to make our own, as an activity. I hope that's okay? They said they had all of the stuff on hand. It seemed like a good idea at the time, but if you don't want to, or if it would make you miss her too much, I'm sure they'll just bring us a normal pasta dish and we can have lunch." I'm rambling nervously but cut off abruptly when he reaches up his left hand and cups my cheek.

"That was very thoughtful of you, and, yes, I would be delighted to make pasta with you today." He looks into my eyes as he says it, and I can see the sincerity there.

"Ok, then—we can just go back to the kitchen and everything should be waiting for us."

He grabs my free hand, and links it through his elbow before leading me through the dining room and into the kitchen. It's my first time being back here, but it looks like a standard industrial kitchen—it's nothing like the dormitory's kitchen where I made my cornbread. I can see off to one side there is a big stainless-steel prep table with a "Reserved" sign, what I can only assume is a pasta machine, and a neat stack of ingredients.

Once we walk up, I can see that they've also included a selection of recipes.

Antonio flips through the provided stack, making faces at a few until he lands on one that suits him. "Here we go! Nothing extra, just the essentials. Good pasta is like a good relationship. A few simple ingredients brought together in just the right way." He kisses his fingertips dramatically, "Perfection!"

He wastes no time handing me an apron and rolling up his sleeves. I do the same, and then he puts me to work measuring and pouring things onto the flat work surface for him. Once everything is piled into a little hill, he goes to work with a fork carefully mixing in the middle. I watch in awe as he brings it all together into a smooth dough without spilling a single drop of egg. After a few moments, he lets me take a turn with the kneading.

"Like this?" I ask, pushing the dough away. Surprisingly, it's not sticky like bread doughs that I've made before.

"No, no—not so hard. Gently, smoothly." He places his hands over mine and shows me how hard to press the dough into the table. We stay like that for a moment or two, before he lets me finish on my own. He takes the dough and wraps it up for me, and we set it aside to relax. While the dough is resting, we flip through the sauce options they've left for us and we let one of the kitchen staff know we'd like to try the ragù. Antonio was skeptical until they assured him they'd started it this morning in preparation for our activity.

With that sorted, we decided to skip the machine altogether and let him teach me how to make pappardelle, which is cut by hand. Once the resting time was over, he demonstrated how to roll and flour the dough, before it was cutting time.

I'm watching him roll the dough out, mesmerized by the smooth repetitive motions, when he brings me back to the matter at hand. "So, Sadie, are you making your choice today? I've heard that you've had two dates so far, and two men have gone home. Am I to be the third?"

Put on the spot, I internally flail for the right words. I'd planned to discuss it with him later, over a big steaming bowl of fresh pasta to soothe our emotions. Not now, before I'd even had my carb fix. "Uhm, well, I am trying to narrow things down today. To be honest, I'm torn on where to go from here." I fiddle with my apron strings, all Zen gone in an instant. The kitchen that felt warm and cozy before is now too hot and full of clanging pots and pans.

He nods once, sharply, "Let's talk about it. What are you thinking? You can be honest with me, you won't hurt my feelings." He continues rolling, giving us something else to focus on.

"Well, with you there is more to consider than the other two men. You have Gianna, and I have to think about her as well." I hesitate, but when he stays silent, I continue, "Plus, you and I have the greatest age difference of any of my matches, and you're not local to Georada."

He looks up quickly, "It's okay, Sadie, I know I'm old. It's not news to me that you're half my age." He sounds lighthearted, and I wish desperately that I felt the same. Twenty-one years is a massive age difference. He's the same age as Gavin, and I've never even considered any of his friends as potential boyfriends, because the distance was just too far. Cade and Teddy on the other hand, now they've got some good-looking buddies. *Not that I'd admit that to them in a million years.*

"You're not old," I say lightly.

"Let's circle back. Gianna, how do you feel about being an instant mother? She's a pre-teen, and I can only assume things get more *interesting* from here on out," he says bluntly.

I stop fidgeting for a moment, really considering it. "You know, it doesn't bother me. She really pulls at my heartstrings, and if I could help her, that would make me happier than anything else I think has come out of this program. Now, whether she'd be as excited to meet me, I can't say."

He stops rolling and wipes a bead of sweat from his forehead before answering. "She'd love you, Sadie, and I really mean that. Ready to learn to cut?"

"Yes! Show me." I watch closely as he dusts, folds, dusts, folds, and then starts cutting the stack neatly into long ribbons.

We work in silence, and in a few short minutes our dough has been transformed into two piles of noodles. His, neat and tidy; mine, a bit more rough-shod. We pass them off to the kitchen staff, who tell us to go pick a table and our lunch will be out shortly.

"I can't wait to try this pasta! I've always wanted to learn to make it," I say excitedly as we choose our table.

He smiles, "You're a natural. It will be great."

Bread arrives, proffered by a uniformed waiter, and we both grab a piece. I nibble at it nervously, but he seems at ease.

"Sadie, I'm going to make this easy on you. I don't feel like you're choosing me. Am I right?" he lays it all out, and looks so calm.

I take a deep breath. "Yes, Antonio, I'm so sorry. I really wanted to give us a shot, especially for Gianna. She deserves someone to talk to the next few years as she goes through the next phase of her life. I would have been lost without my mother at her age." I stop, the lump in my throat preventing further conversation. I look down at my water glass, unsure what else to say.

"It's okay, Sadie. You and I are not quite meant to be. But I'd like to propose something, if you're willing to consider it." He steeples his fingers together. "Would you be willing to speak with Gianna, maybe just as a friend? You're going through so much, I do understand if the answer is no. But there aren't many girls her age, and no one I trust as much as you to steer her well."

"I would love that, truly! I don't know when I'll be allowed, but as soon as the program lets us make outside calls again, I'd be happy to talk with her. Maybe we could set up a recurring phone date, in case she has questions about things?" I suggest.

A genuine smile crosses his features, "That would be perfect. You truly are a good girl, Sadie. One of those two ducks is going to be lucky to have you."

I chuckle at his proclamation as our waiter reappears with our pasta, which smells divine. I take my first bite, and it feels like the gates of heaven opened and delivered this pasta dish directly to us. *Thank you, pasta Jesus. Thank you.*

"This is so good," I mumble, my mouth is full but it's too delicious to stop eating to talk.

Antonio laughs, and we go on discussing pasta sauce-making techniques, and what he'd recommend if I want to recreate this bowl of heaven at a later date. At the end of the meal, he writes his phone number down on a napkin, and slides it over to me for safe-keeping. We part with a hug outside of the women's dorm, and I'm happy to know it's not the last I'll hear from him. He truly is a kind soul.

SEVENTEEN
CONTENDERS

I make a snap decision; something about the finality of being down to just two contenders has brought me new clarity. I cancel both remaining dates that were scheduled for the day, and instead set up one new date with both men. Bowling, at the sports center, and I invite Teddy and Faith. I need my brother's opinion, and I'm a little ashamed I haven't considered it sooner. Being away from my family has shaken me in a lot of ways, made me feel isolated, even when surrounded by all these people.

My tablet dings twice in quick succession. Faith accepted, and Matthew. I head into the bathroom to do something a little better with my hair, since Faith always goes all out. Not that it's a competition, but, I also don't want to get shown-up in front of my future husband. *Whoever that is.*

I flip on some music recommended by the ever-rocking Jenna, and go to work on my unruly brunette head. I think curls, something flirty but polished, would be best. Feeling the rumble of monster butterflies in my stomach, I spend more time primping than I have the entire time I've been here. Very, very soon I'll be saying "I do" with one of these guys. My mind spins over the two men, trying to analyze them fairly, logically.

Matthew is handsome; he's tall and all straight lines, sharp edges. His look fits his personality, as he's also direct, to the point, and doesn't BS; all of which I appreciate. He isn't local, but he's said before that he'd be willing to split time between York where his businesses are, and Georada where my family is. He's got the money to make that feasible, and probably a lot more, though I don't really care about that.

Fancy dinners and fancier homes and cars aren't my bag. I already had everything I wanted, right back home in Georada—land, clean air, family, friendship, my amazing Morgan. I set down the curling iron, and stare myself down in the mirror for a minute. Is that *really* all I want out of life, though? I always assumed I'd find "the one" someday, have that fairy tale, swept-off-your-feet, love-at-first-sight kind of romance that my parents did. The one who lasts forever, the one who completes me, makes me a better person. If I'm being honest, I do still want that.

I pick the curling iron back up and contemplate Patrick. He's handsome, with his dark, thick hair and working-man muscles. He's not quite as refined as Matthew, a bit rougher around the edges, but more in a boyish way than an unkempt way. He's shown himself to be caring and protective throughout my time here, and let's not forget he literally took a man's life to save mine, without a second thought. Granted, it's his job. But I have the feeling that there's more to it than that—more to our connection.

Which isn't to say there's no connection to Matthew. He's powerful, warm, and—despite the fact that I'm sure many would consider him intimidating—he treats me as an equal. There's something to be said about a man who has the world at his feet, but still knows how to treat people. He's never once been derogatory or unkind to a waiter here, and he's never acted bored when I talk about my home life or interest in horses and ranching. With Matthew, I do worry that he'd be disappointed with me in time, and that's something I need to have a real discussion with him about. I'm a simple woman at heart, and that's not going to change no matter how much money he has. I'm never going to be a perfectly tweezed trophy wife, and I'm always going to want to live close to the land. The question is, can he accept me as I am, or does he want to turn me into a Margaret?

I finish my curls and set the curling iron to the side to apply some seldom-used makeup. Then it's on to my nicest pair of dark skinny jeans, dress boots, and a black top. I'm inspecting myself in my closet's full-length mirror when I hear a soft knock on the door, barely audible over my getting ready jams. I walk over and open it to find Faith waiting with a huge smile on her face.

"Sadie! You finally want to double date with us!" She grabs me into an unexpected hug, and I pat her back awkwardly until she releases me.

"Yeah, of course. I should have thought of it sooner, but, I've been distracted." I stammer, unsure what else to say.

"It's okay, I'm just glad you're finally okay with it!" she enthuses.

"Come in, come in. And, of course I'm okay with it, why wouldn't I be?" I ask, confused.

She bites her lip before answering me, "Well, a lot of the girls have gone on double dates, but you haven't, even though your brother is here. And we could both tell up front that you weren't thrilled he'd signed up. We agreed to just give you some space, and hopefully you'd ask us when you were ready. I'm just so glad you're ready now!" She flings her arms back around me before I can even shut the door.

We repeat the hug-and-back-pat routine before she finally lets me go and wanders into my room. "So, who are we going with tonight? Hunk-a-hunk-a-burning Matthew, or the mysterious Mr. Patrick?"

"Err, well, both?" She spins back to face me, and her face lights up. "I need some outside opinions. And who better than you and Teddy?"

She claps twice, "Oh, excellent idea. Your brother will be thrilled to grill those two tonight!"

I groan, "No! No grilling, I just need, I don't know, someone else to see them both together, with me, and tell me who to pick. I'm torn in so many directions and I just don't know what to do. I need someone else to decide." I flop on the end of my bed, sprawled out and staring at the ceiling.

She sits on the bench, and wiggles my booted foot. "Sadie, I am excited to finally try out this whole "sisters" thing, but I don't think siblings usually pick each other's spouses." She releases my foot.

"Ugh, why not?" I complain.

"Okay, well, let's just do this date and then we can talk girl talk after. Are you ready?"

"Mostly, I'm just not sure about this shirt. I don't really have anything fancy. I feel like I need to step it up a little, and this is the best I packed." I sit up, and smooth my hair back from my face.

She looks me up and down, "Hold on a second, I'll be right back." She heads out the door, leaving it flapping open behind her.

I get up, turn off my music, and she's already back, holding something black and sparkly in her hands. She shoves it at me.

"Go put this on, and let's go! We don't want to keep our men waiting." She shoos me into the bathroom.

Moving quickly, I pull off my top and pull on its much more sparkly cousin, who is much lower cut. I quickly adjust my cleavage, and make sure I'm firmly tucked in. I give myself one last perusal in the mirror, taking in my brunette curls, blue eyes, and pale skin. I feel like I clean up okay; hopefully the guys agree.

Exiting the bathroom, Faith is waiting with hands on hips. "Much better!" she says, before grabbing my arm and hauling me out of the room. I manage to get the door shut and locked behind us, barely.

She rolls her eyes, "Why are you so worried about the door? There's nobody in here but us girls."

My brain flips back to the day on the porch, hearing Eric in somebody's room. "I'll tell you later, but you're not going to believe me."

"Ooh, juicy!" she quips as we make our way down the stairs.

I can't help but notice how much more chipper the girl beside me is than the one who showed up that first day here. I wonder what's changed. Does she actually have feelings for Teddy, too? That possibility makes my heart happy; they both deserve a chance at real love.

We quickly make our way past the main hall, and follow the stone-lined walking-path to the sports center. Faith pushes the door open, and we are instantly greeted with the sounds of cheering male voices coming from one of the mini sports theaters.

"There must be a game on," I observe.

Faith ignores me in lieu of heading straight for the bowling lanes, still pulling me by the arm.

"Faith, if I didn't know better, I'd say you're excited to see my brother tonight," I test the waters.

She shrugs one shoulder, but I see a hint of a blush creeping up her neck that can't be denied.

"Oh, my gosh," I stop stock still in the middle of the hallway, "Are you falling for Teddy? Like, for *real* falling for Teddy?"

There's that lip bite again, and she looks nervously at me.

"You ARE! Oh, my gosh, Faith, that's amazing!" Now I surprise her with a spontaneous hug. "Is that the real reason you wanted to go ahead and have the wedding?!" I ask as I pull back.

Her eyes drop, "Sadie, you cannot say anything to him, okay? Promise me you won't! I don't want him to spook and pull back. He's so genuine and kind and just, I don't know, better than any other guy I've met. I don't want to do something to ruin it, okay?"

She looks way more anxious than excited, so I try to rein it in. "Okay, I won't say anything; but, I don't think he'd freak." She nods, and grabs my elbow again, but with more reserve this time.

We arrive at the bowling lanes, and the three men are all standing with their hands in their pockets, not speaking. *This is off to a grand start* I think drily.

Patrick is the first to break the standoff, and steps forward with a smile, "Hey ladies! Looking beautiful this evening." He holds his arms out for a hug, which I briefly accept. I turn to Matthew, and give him a hug also.

"You look breathtaking," he says as we part.

I give him a smile, "Thank you. You look really nice too." And he does, in clinging jeans and boat shoes, with a gray button-up shirt with the top button undone. His eyes are dark chocolate, warm and deep, and his hair is always done just so. It does make a girl wonder if he wakes up looking so perfect.

I blink, unsure what else to say. A wave of uncertainty rolls over me, second-guessing if this was really a good idea to invite my last two matches on the same date. Hopefully there's no macho man drama.

Teddy rubs his hands together excitedly next to Faith, "All right, how are we doing this? Individuals? Teams? Guys vs. girls?"

Patrick weighs in, "Let's do teams. It's more fun that way."

"Are we going to play two on three?" Matthew objects.

"No, we can just count Sadie's score twice—once for each of us. So, three teams," Patrick offers.

Matthew levels him with an intense gaze, "Fine. May the best match win."

Teddy breaks the tension with an evil cackle, "You two are screwed! Sadie sucks at bowling!" He grabs Faith by the arm, "Come on, lets go get you a ball."

"I do not suck at bowling! You just always team me up with Phil and he's a terrible bowling partner!" I retort and roll my eyes. "Why did I invite my brother on this date again?"

Both Patrick and Matthew are looking at me appraisingly. "What?" I ask.

They look at each other, and Patrick is the first one to speak up, "It's nice to see you with your brother. You seem lighter, more relaxed. I'm glad you're able to have him here with you."

"I was just trying to imagine you with six Teddys at one time," Matthew says.

"Did it break your brain? You should see us on Founding Day; Mom roasts two whole turkeys and she practically has to beat them all out of the kitchen with a stick." I smile at the happy memory.

"What do you make on Founding Day?" Patrick asks.

"Oh, I usually do all the baking. So, cornbread or rolls, and then a pound cake, because that's my dad's favorite. Oh! And, sometimes, a chocolate pecan pie. I don't really like it, but my brothers will fight over the last piece like wolves."

"That's a lot of baking. You must be really good," he says. "I'd love to confirm that for myself, but you never did make me those cookies," he teases.

Matthew raises one eyebrow before cutting in, "Should we go pick a ball for you?"

"Yes! Let's go."

The three of us walk over to a half-wall lined with balls in all different colors and sizes. I choose a bright pink six-pound ball. The guys both pick much heavier ones, and then we head back to the lane. Teddy is already selecting our teams on the touchscreen. He's named them "Teddy's Triumph," "Matt Attack," and "Patrick the Pulverizer."

I snort, but he just grins at me. Conversation flows pretty well once we get into a groove, and it's all light banter. The awkwardness eases away by my second turn to bowl, and I even make a spare, which is good for me. Doing my standard victory dance, I turn around to see the whole group staring at me. Faith is the first one to laugh, and I just stick my tongue out and dance again. It feels good to let loose, be normal.

Our game goes pretty quickly, and the guys have all got competitive streaks a mile wide. Teddy and Faith are cute together, all politeness and small sideways glances. He's in full gentleman mode, which Mom would be delighted to see. My mom will absolutely adore Faith, when they finally get to meet.

The first game ends with Matthew and me in first place, followed by Teddy and Faith, and then Patrick and me in last.

"I demand a rematch! We're just getting warmed up," Teddy declares, resetting the scoreboard for round two. Round two is well under way when Faith asks me where I want to go for my honeymoon.

"Uhm, I don't know. To be honest, I haven't really thought of it yet. Where are you two going to go?"

"We were thinking either Jamaica, or maybe somewhere further north where it's cooler. Maybe Mairmont? Eat lobster, go sailing, enjoy the cold."

"Oh, I have heard Mairmont is gorgeous this time of year. Once you choose a place, are you locked in to stay there until you go to a pregnancy center?" I ask.

Faith shakes her head, "No, you can request a transfer after three months, but most people stay put. The resorts are pretty nice, and you get into a daily groove."

"That makes sense. Where do you two think you'd want to go?" I pose the question to my matches, realizing we've not discussed the honeymoon. I think I've been blocking out the next phase of this program, but I need to pull my head out of the sand.

Patrick looks thoughtful, but Matthew has an immediate answer, "I'd prefer Mairmont, just because it's closer to York. It would be much more convenient if I had to fly out for meetings on non-fertile weeks."

I'm floored by his response. I didn't think it was an option to leave the honeymoon. And is he already thinking about fertile weeks? My face heats. *Of course he is, that's the whole point, Sadie.*

Patrick comes to my rescue, "I'm down for anywhere! I've always loved travel when I've had the chance to do it."

"Well, we'd like to all decide together, so we can go to the same place. It's really important to Teddy to stay with you as much as possible in this process. I think the Mairmont location actually has a pregnancy center on site, so whoever gets pregnant first can stay on location until the other does, too, and is ready to come back to Georada." She pauses, and I can see the hope in her eyes, "Or York, I guess. I've heard they've got top-of-the-line fertility and pregnancy centers, too," she adds, looking at Matthew.

Teddy finishes his turn, and walks up, "I'm another vote for the Mairmont resort. It'd be nice to go somewhere with snow for awhile, instead of all this heat."

"Mairmont it is!" Patrick agrees with a smile. Matthew shoots him a look, and tension starts to rise again. You can practically feel the testosterone between the two of them, and I'm anxious for an escape.

"My turn!" Standing quickly, I grab my pink ball, happy to get out of the conversation, even temporarily. My concentration is crap, and I only hit two pins.

Matthew frowns at the scoreboard, as Teddy and Faith take the lead from us. Teddy pumps his fist in the air, then grabs Faith and plants a kiss on her temple.

"That's what I'm talking about! Way to hand it to us, Sadie!"

I'll take the ribbing if it means the end of the honeymoon conversation. Thankfully, it's Matthew's turn, and the talk returns to random bowling chatter. But my brain won't stop turning over the reality of what's about to happen.

After a few more turns, I ask Faith, "So, have you picked a wedding day?"

"Well, we were hoping for this Friday. But we don't want to rush you into choosing, so, we can wait for next month if you're still on the fence." Her voice drops lower at the end, not wanting to draw the guys' attention.

"I really don't want you two to wait around on me; it's not fair to keep you on hold when you've already waited so long," I respond, my gaze flicking back and forth between the two men.

They are so opposite, and whoever I choose is going to steer my life down a completely different path. The question is, which path do I want to be on? "You should schedule it for Friday. I'm going to choose by then," I say firmly, and Faith's jaw drops.

"Are you sure? We really want you to take your time and get comfortable. Teddy is very firm on not abandoning you here. He keeps saying Cade will kick his butt if he lets you out of his sight."

"Well, I'll make it easy on him. I'll set a date for Friday, too. And then we'll all head to Mairmont together."

"Wait, you want to get married Friday?" Patrick interjects, and Matthew whips around. "*This* Friday?" he repeats.

I nod, "I think it's time, don't you?" I meet his eyes, and he looks back searchingly. After a moment he recognizes my resolve, and gives me a nod. I flick my gaze to Matthew, and he looks calculating.

"Are you sure you're ready to make that decision?" he asks, and I can hear his skepticism.

"Yes, I am." All four of them stare at me, as if I'm about to sprout another head. "I'm not going to make some big announcement right now, I need to sleep on it. But, tomorrow; I promise. And then Friday we'll have two weddings."

Teddy lets out a loud breath, and slaps both of the other guys on the shoulder. "Well, I hope neither of you have cold feet, because it's about to get real up in here." He winks at me. "And while I hate to change the subject, I'd love to point out that Faith and I just won round two, and I think we're ready to call it a night. I'll let you two escort my sister wherever she'd like to head next." He gives me a peck on the cheek before absconding with Faith.

"Shall we all grab a bite to eat?" Matthew suggests amiably.

"I'm down for that," Patrick agrees, and they both look to me expectantly.

"Sure, sounds good." They flank me as we exit the sports center to the sound of hollering from the sports theater. "What is going on in there?" I mutter.

"Ice hockey." Matthew states, and I can see the longing in his eyes.

We make our way in silence to the Main Hall, and request a table for three. The host seats us, and a waiter brings us drinks shortly afterwards. I'm glancing back and forth between Matthew and Patrick, hoping one of them will start a neutral conversation when Elena appears at our table with Hector in tow.

"SADIE! Did you hear the new gossip?" she asks, eyes dancing.

"No? Good gossip or bad gossip?" Surely word of our impending double wedding hasn't spread already?

"Oh, it's not good, that's for sure," she says, her voice a hair quieter, "Apparently one of the female nurses' routine medical exams came back with an STD. Can you believe that? These people preach about no illegal relationships, and one of the staff is clearly having one!"

I'm surprised, but not shocked. "How did you come upon this information, exactly?"

"Oh, well, you will have it, too, when you get back to the dormitory. There's an announcement that an extra round of testing has been called for everyone on the premises. Apparently, if one person tests positive they make *everyone* test, unless they divulge the relationship."

Matthew remarks drily, "Apparently this nurse can keep her mouth shut, if not her knees."

I smack him on the arm, "Matthew! That's an awful thing to say."

He shrugs, "It's true, regardless. Whoever tests positive with her is going to be in a world of hurt. The punishments are pretty severe for fraternization outside an approved relationship."

"What if she's not married? I know it's not a sanctioned relationship, but if she's old enough to be out of the program she shouldn't get punished," I argue, feeling bad for the mystery nurse.

"Didn't you read the emergency declaration a few weeks back, to the Compulsory Marriage and Reproduction Act? Any woman under the age of forty-five who isn't already married with children has to report for fertility testing. That's probably why she was getting tested," Patrick informs me.

"I read it, but I must have missed that." My stomach sinks. The new laws are more and more restrictive, like a collective noose tightening around the neck of every woman in the NAA.

Hector breaks in, "Ok, Elena, you told them. Let's let them get back to their dinner."

She sighs but follows him out.

"You said the penalties are harsh—what will they do if they find out someone is in an illegal relationship?" I direct the question to Matthew.

"It varies, but if you're enrolled in the compulsory marriage program and they find out you've strayed, you can have a monetary fine, or get sent to a correctional institution."

"That doesn't sound good," I wonder if that's where they sent Josephine?

"Best not to find out firsthand," Patrick agrees.

Our food arrives, and a weighty silence has fallen over the table. We eat the provided enchiladas mostly in silence. When we're finished, Matthew kisses me on the cheek and then takes his leave to go make a business call, so Patrick walks me back to my dormitory.

Our fingers are lightly linked, and we stop at the bottom of the stairs.

"Now that it's just the two of us, there's something I need to tell you," Patrick says, voice serious.

"Okay, is everything all right?" He has me worried.

"I'm not sure, but I wanted to give you an update. You know Glitch looked into Josephine's whereabouts but wasn't able to find her, right?"

I nod, and he continues. "Well, apparently he set an alert on her name, so that he'd get notified if she popped back into the system at any time. Kind of like a digital warrant. Well, she showed up today."

I gasp, "Where is she? Is she at a correctional facility?"

He shifts, and runs his hand through his hair, "No, she's not."

"That's a good thing, right? What aren't you telling me?" I search his face, as if an answer is going to appear there if I look hard enough.

"Well, I'm not exactly sure. But the record that showed up is a pregnancy notice. She was transferred to the Mairmont pregnancy center this morning." He falls silent, pensive.

My mouth falls open, "So they made her marry that guy, and she's already pregnant? That's insanely fast! It's only been a few weeks—how is it even possible to get pregnant and know it that fast?" My mind is spinning.

He shakes his head, "No, that's the thing. Glitch, as you know, doesn't necessarily follow the rules to get the information he does, and—well, he says the record isn't normal. There's no accompanying marriage record, and if it weren't for the alert he set up he wouldn't have been able to find it through normal channels."

"What does that mean, exactly? There has to be a marriage record somewhere, right?"

"I don't know what it means. Glitch is trying to dig more, but the information that's available is really sparse. He loves a challenge, though, so I'm sure he'll figure it out." He looks at me with a grim expression. "I don't want to sway your decision, but I think Mairmont is the best option for the honeymoon choice if you want a chance to find Josephine." He rakes his hand through his hair again, and it falls back in a messy pile.

"Thank you for telling me. Yes, we definitely need to get to Mairmont." My burning desire to find out what happened to Josephine won't allow any other choice.

Now it's his turn to search my eyes, "We? As in, *we* we, or uh —" he lets the question fade off, dangling into the void.

I swallow, and look at my feet. How to broach this topic? "Uhm . . ." My fingers twist together behind me of their own accord.

"Oh, I see. Well, I'll let you get on up to bed then." He looks away, but I can see the sadness etching itself into his handsome face.

"No! Wait! Yes, we as in us, we." The words stumble out in an inelegant rush. What is it about Patrick that always leaves me in a tangle? Mind, heart, words.

He holds very still, and assesses me without speaking, waiting for me to say more.

"I don't know how to do this, but . . . I think I am going to release Matthew in the morning. I mean, that is, assuming you're okay with that and marrying me and trying to have a baby. I mean, you're in the program so I assume you're still in, but I'm probably not what you were expecting. It seemed like we were doing well and you would be happy to marry me, but you can tell me now and I can release you instead if you prefer.

I would understand; we still don't know each other that well and you're really handsome so you could probably have your pick of girls. Well, if girls were still allowed to pick. Oh, my Lord, would you please say something?" I stop the wreck that is my train of thought.

A smile gradually replaces the sadness on his face, and he reaches forward to cup my cheek in his warm hand. "Sadie, were you by chance just trying to tell me that you want to have my babies?"

I smack him lightly on the chest, and he chuckles before growing serious. Then, right there on the walkway in front of the dormitory, he sinks to one knee in front of me. He grasps my hands in his, and my heart flutters. Is he doing what I think he's doing?

"Sadie, beautiful, sweet Sadie. You are a kind, loving, spitfire of a woman. You have the biggest heart and the most intense spirit of anyone I've ever known. Would you do me the greatest honor of becoming my wife?" He looks up at me with a solemn expression, and I can feel myself shaking like a leaf in a hurricane.

"I, uhm . . . Wow, I wasn't expecting that at all," I say, and my voice shakes.

His lips quirk up in a half-grin, "Should I take it back?"

"No! I mean, yes, I will marry you! Please don't take it back." I stop the train wreck of words, and think carefully before admitting, "I wanted it to be you, before I even knew you were an option." The full force of his smile hits me like a ton of bricks, and he stands in one fluid motion and wraps me in a hug. I hug him back, and the shaking starts to subside. We stay there like that, and for a small eternity it feels like there are only the two of us in this whole screwed up world.

EIGHTEEN
REVELATIONS

T he next morning, after going in for my mandatory STD test, I invite Matthew to meet in the courtyard between our dorms. He's dressed in a suit, and his face is impossible to read. I tell him what I've decided, and he doesn't look surprised.

"Following your heart I see," he says, his voice barely audible over the anxious pounding of my pulse.

I nod, "I hope you know that I felt something for you too, Matt. I didn't keep you here so long to lead you on. It just . . . well, you and I live very different lives. I may never be the wife you need, and I don't know if you'd ever be content back home with my family. You are a great guy, I just don't think our lives are compatible—even if our genes are."

He reaches out his fingertips and brushes them against my bottom lip, soft as a feather, just once. He smiles, but the sadness is clear in his tone, "For you I would have tried." He clears his throat, and the businessman façade slides back into place.

I don't know what else to say, so I just give him a sad smile in return.

"Well, my helicopter will be here momentarily. If you're ever in York, feel free to look me up. I'd love to hear how things are going." He says it briskly, as if I'm a business acquaintance.

"Yes, I definitely will." I say. I give him one final wave and then head over to the main hall for breakfast.

When I arrive at the dining hall, I see all the remaining girls lined up at one long table. It reminds me of my very first day, when we stopped for those tacos on our way here. Some of the faces have changed, but here we are again, back on the precipice of a huge life change. I grab an empty seat.

"I'm just saying, I'm ready. I don't see the point in waiting months more to get this show on the road, get knocked up, and get this over with. My next fertile phase is in three weeks. I'm going to ask him to schedule the wedding three days before. Rip off the band-aid!" Jenna pronounces.

"Marcus will be so thrilled to hear that you think sex with him will be like ripping off a bandage." Margaret says primly, while dabbing at her lipstick with a cloth napkin.

Jenna snorts, "Well, they say it hurts the first time, so, if the bandage fits . . ."

Faith chuckles, "You'll all be fine! It's over before you know it. Now, I'd like to change the subject to some news, now that Sadie has joined us." She pauses for effect. "We're getting married tomorrow!"

"Congratulations!" Leigh says with sincere excitement.

"Yeah, that's awesome Faith, Teddy seems like a great guy," Elena says, glancing at me to gauge my reaction.

"Darn straight!" I agree with the sentiment, and I hope my encouragement will ease any fears Faith might have lingering about her acceptance into our family.

Faith looks at me pointedly, and it takes me a minute to realize what she's getting at. As I'm about to share the news, chopper blades can be heard overhead.

"What is that?" Charlotte asks, sounding worried.

"Oh, Lord have mercy, please don't let it be more kidnappers." Jenna says with irritation.

"Uh, guys, I don't think it's kidnappers." I raise my voice just enough so they can hear me better, before the noise cuts off. "It's Matthew. He called a chopper to take him back to York." I look down at my lap, and smooth a non-existent wrinkle on my well-worn blue jeans.

"Did you release him, too?" Charlotte asks softly.

I nod, "Patrick and I are going to be getting married. Tomorrow," I add, that last bit almost as an afterthought.

"Oh my gawd, you chose!" Nell blurts out.

"Took you long enough," Margaret says, haughty as usual.

I roll my eyes, not willing to engage with her today.

"I chose!" I address Nell, who is shoveling hash browns into her mouth.

Nell doesn't stop chewing to ask, "Why the rush? I mean, I get why this one is ready to go," she points a thumb at Faith, "but why are you so Johnny-on-the-spot? Can't wait to get your hands on Patrick-hottie-O'Roarke?"

I chuckle, "No, it's not that. Teddy doesn't want to go until I do, so I'm going, too. No sense holding up the lovebirds." I tease Faith, who blushes again. "Besides, what's the point in dragging it out? When are you and Atlas going to get hitched?"

She chews as she considers, "Probably soon. I'm not in a rush, but he's finally won me over. He's not as scary as I originally thought. Well, to me anyways. It's kind of nice to have all those muscles on my side for a change." She spears a breakfast sausage and pops it into her mouth behind the potatoes.

"Ugh, we do *not* need to see your food. What are you, twelve? Have some class," Margaret says.

The waiter arrives at the table with a steaming plate of breakfast for me, so I dig in and the conversation moves on to what kind of dress Faith is going to wear, and what she chose the first two times. I'm only half listening when our table is approached by the ever personable Dr. Mitch. Eric is trailing behind him, but for once he's not a walking toothpaste ad. He looks so concerned, I set my fork down and await their news. This can't be good.

"Excuse me, Margaret, I need you to come with us," Dr. Mitch says in a cool tone.

Margaret gives him a once-over, taking in Eric standing to the side, "What is this in regard to, Doctor?"

"I think we'd better discuss that privately."

"Ooh, Miss Perfect's in trouble," Elena jokes.

I'm not laughing, taking in the look on the doctor's face. Something is wrong.

"Would you shut up! You're all so childish! I swear, I can't wait to be away from all of you." Margaret seethes at Elena as she slams her napkin to the table and rises, causing the silverware to rattle in protest against the breakfast plates.

"Doctor, I already did my testing this morning, ridiculous as it was for you to require that *again*. What more could you possibly want with me?" She puts a hand on her hip, and glares at him.

He is not swayed by her attitude, "I wish you'd have agreed to do this privately, but fine, if you insist on making a public scene, we can. Eric here has tested positive for the same STD as nurse Carolyn. He has provided a list of all his sexual partners, and you are one of the names on the list." Gasps come from the whole table, and the color drains from Margaret's face as she looks to Eric, who's looking at his shoes. "Now, if you will please come with me, I'd like to discuss your necessary treatment in private, and then the program director will need to discuss the ramifications of this situation with all of the involved parties." He looks nonplussed, and gestures towards the doorway.

Margaret looks around at us all gaping in shock, and storms past Dr. Mitch and Eric. As she walks by, Eric tries to grab her arm.

"Don't you lay a filthy finger on me, you pompous, no-good PRICK!" She snatches her arm away and flees out the door.

We all watch in shocked silence as they exit the dining room. After a beat, Jenna says, "Dude." We all look around the table in disbelief. "I mean, *Eric*? She was hooking up with the cruise director? I'm almost proud—I never would have guessed she had it in her."

"I guess that answers the question of whose room I heard him in a while back," I muse.

"Shut the front door!" Leigh blurts, "You knew he was hooking up with someone in the dorms, and didn't say anything?" She's stopped mid-stir of her coffee to gape at me.

"Well, I didn't *know*, know. I heard him say something suggestive and I assumed, but I didn't know whose room he was in." I give them a shrug.

"Yeah, but how do you just sit on that kind of juicy info and not spill it?" Leigh shakes her head, as if the idea of not immediately sharing something is a foreign concept. *If only she knew.*

I just shrug a shoulder, "If something's not mine to share, I really try not to. Plus, I wouldn't have wanted to get one of you into trouble."

"I wonder what her match is going to do when he finds out? They aren't scheduled for a wedding date yet, and he might be able to back out based on grounds of infidelity and unfit health now," Charlotte says, ever the caring one even when Margaret has been so unkind to her.

"Her dad's some important politician in South Georada, I doubt he'll let him weasel out of marrying her over a little cheating. I mean, I feel for the guy, but Margaret doesn't play. You think Daddy Dearest is going to lay down like a kitten when his daughter's reputation is on the line?" Jenna says, sarcasm thick.

"Her family will probably have to pay a fine, but I don't think they'll let her out of her match," I speculate, remembering last night's conversation about the program's penalties.

We finish up breakfast, and speculations continue flying over who else was on Eric's list, and what's going to happen to all of them. I can't really get into it with thoughts of Josephine's mystery situation plaguing the back of my mind. While I sincerely hope Margaret gets just a slap-on-the-wrist fine, there's no hard and fast rule. And I'm not rooting for any woman to end up on the wrong side of this program's penal system.

I decide to see if Patrick is available to discuss the wedding and make some choices with me, and he responds "yes" almost instantly and asks me to meet him at the pond with my mini-tablet so we can go over the details.

A brisk walk later, I arrive to find him waiting for me with a smile, and I see he's set up a pretty blue picnic blanket with a plate of chocolate-covered strawberries settled in the middle. His handsome face draws me in like a moth to a flame, and I can't help but smile back at him. He's wearing his guard uniform, but he looks at ease.

"Were you on duty?" I ask. "I hope I didn't interrupt something important." I hope he doesn't mind my asking him to meet me so out of the blue.

"Today is my last day, actually. Most of your matches had to put their jobs on hold at the beginning of the process, so they kept me longer than expected. I'll be off with you indefinitely, so you did me a favor, springing me a little early." He gives me a hug, and I lean my ear against his chest, and am lulled for a moment by the beat of his heart. He places a gentle kiss on the top of my head before stepping back from the hug, but he doesn't release me.

"So, we're doing this thing, huh? Tomorrow?"

I nod, "Yes, if you're still okay with that plan? Teddy won't set the date unless I do, too. He's worried I'll get kidnapped and he won't be here," I admit.

"I can't blame him, I wouldn't leave you either. But I won't let anything happen to you Sadie, I hope you know that. No matter what, I'll protect you." His voice is determined. He takes my hand and leads me to the blanket. Once I'm settled down, he sits next to me, close enough for me to feel the heat radiating from him, but not quite touching.

"So, what do we need to hammer out?" he asks, getting straight down to business.

I pull up the tablet, and open the Bachelor Book. Faith told me that as soon as I requested a date, I'd be sent a questionnaire with all our wedding and honeymoon preferences. She did hers last night, but I'd wanted to wait for Patrick. It's his wedding too, after all. I click it, and select the "schedule wedding" option.

It's surreal; just over a month ago I run into this man in the halls, and hope my match is half as good looking as him. And now I'm sitting on a beautiful afternoon date, planning to marry him tomorrow. It's almost too good to be true. I think of Leigh with her match that's more than twice her age, and James the politician that I let go early on. Not to mention *Spencer*. It could have gone way, way worse. I feel a deep gratitude that despite how we came together, that I'm sitting on this blanket with someone who's kind, honest, and genuine.

He reaches over and brushes his fingertip across my knuckles, "Having second thoughts already? I thought you were supposed to wait for that until right before you walk down the aisle to me, so you can make a dramatic escape in your running shoes and gown," he jokes.

I roll my eyes, "Have you been watching old movies? I'm not going to run away. I hear the place is guarded anyways; I don't think I'd get very far." I look at him pointedly, and rake my eyes down his guard's uniform.

That pulls a deep chuckle out of him, and his eyes lock with mine. He leans in, and I hold my breath as his lips meet mine. The kiss starts out gentle, innocent. His lips mold to mine, and his hand wraps around to the back of my neck underneath my braid. The sudden contact makes me shiver, and he deepens the kiss. His other hand comes around my back, and slides down low, just above the waist of my jeans. I'm entranced by the small circles he's drawing there with his thumb. The spell is broken, however, when the hand on my neck slides down my shoulder and grazes the edge of my bra. I stiffen, and he drops his hand and pulls it back as if I'd burned him.

"I'm sorry, I—" I start to stammer, but he stops me with a gentle finger to the lips.

"Don't ever apologize. We're in no hurry, and nothing is going to happen that you're uncomfortable with, not ever. Deal?" His face is sincere, and I relax again. Once I nod, he continues, "You can always talk to me, tell me what you want and when. Or how, okay? We're building a relationship here, and it has to work for both of us. I have no desire to rush it to check off one more baby for the marriage program a month sooner, do you?"

Blushing, I shake my head and look down. I can't find the words for this conversation just yet.

His thumb grazes over my knuckles again, and I enjoy the simple contact. "Let's get our wedding planned. What's on this list?"

Back on track, I pick the tablet up from where it slid onto the blanket, and we get to work. Time, venue, colors, flowers, musical theme, dinner preference, the whole she-bang in one simple list. It takes about an hour, but then it's done. Wedding planning: check.

I set the tablet down, but it dings almost immediately with a notification. I pick it up, and it says my wedding dresses are being delivered to my suite.

He bites into a strawberry, and I watch the juice slide down his chin as if my life depends on it, before he captures it with a finger. He catches my stare, and I can feel myself heating up again. I quickly stand, putting some distance between us.

"Well, I guess I'd better go figure out what I'm going to wear tomorrow." I'm reluctant, not wanting our afternoon to end but also starting to feel the nerves. *I'm getting married tomorrow.*

He stands also, and gives me a quick hug before wrapping up the last few strawberries. He walks me back to the dormitory, and we say our goodbyes until tomorrow. "Don't eat these in the dress," he jokes as he hands me the strawberries.

"Really, you don't think red juice and chocolate smears go well with white satin?" I tease back.

He just shakes his head as he gives me one final wave and leaves to go try on his tux. I drag myself up the stairs and through the front door of the dormitory. The click of the latch has an odd finality to it. If all goes well, this will be my last night here, and then I'll be a married woman, heading for my honeymoon. I shiver as the butterflies take flight in my stomach. Ready or not, I'm getting married tomorrow.

NINETEEN

WEDDING BELL BLUES

The day dawns like any other. The sun peeks around my heavy curtains, and I could almost believe it's just another day at the NLC—dates, gossiping girls, and riding Hercules. But, it's not. Today is *the* day. The day my life changes again. The day I become Mrs. Sadie O'Roarke. Maybe Taylor-O'Roarke. Sadie Ann Taylor O'Roarke. It's long, but it has a nice ring to it.

I stretch, and right on cue the wind chimes of my alarm start to play. I guess it's time to get up and do this thing, as Patrick put it yesterday. Sitting up on the side of the bed, I flick the alarm on my screen to turn it off. Before I can even make my way to the bathroom, there is a boisterous knock on the door. With a groan, I make my way over.

"What is it with you people and visiting at the butt crack of dawn?" I grumble, not caring who's out there.

A surprised Charlotte stands on the other side, holding a steaming cup of hot cocoa, and a small box with a green velvet bow. "Uh, good morning Sadie," she says cautiously. "This is the first time I've seen you before you've had a few minutes to get moving. Not much of a morning person?" she observes.

"Not really. What's up, Charlotte? Do you want to come in?" I give a vague gesture toward the room behind me, and she nods before stepping in.

"I understand my instructions a little more this morning. Patrick told me to give you this," she hands over the steaming mug, which is full of hot cocoa and floating marshmallows, "then wait five minutes and let you open this." She waves the little box, but doesn't hand it over.

I take a sip and groan, happily this time. Chocolate goodness hits me like a wave. "He must have made this; it definitely didn't come from a box," I murmur, going back for a second sip.

She smiles, "He seems like a very thoughtful guy. You take your time, and I'll just wait over there." She takes herself to my bench and sits down.

I make my way into the bathroom, and go through my morning routine while sipping the delicious cocoa. Somewhere towards the last third of the cup, I've become better company than when poor Charlotte first arrived. I make my way out of the bathroom, teeth and hair brushed, and sit across from her in my desk chair. I drain the last precious sips of cocoa, and set down the mug.

The smile she gives me is bright, despite the less-than-warm reception she received initially. "Feeling better? Ready for phase two?"

"Yes, I'm sorry. I am really not a fan of mornings. Three in the afternoon is my jam," I admit, feeling sheepish.

Her laugh is light as she waves me off. "No problem, girl. Here's your present." Handing over the box, she leans back and scooches her hands under her legs.

"Did he tell you what this is?" I ask, nervous to open it.

"Nope, I'm as curious as you. I don't think it'll bite though, whatever it is." She's watching intently.

I pull gently on the soft velvet ribbon, and it comes free in one smooth motion. Setting it aside, I lift the white lid off of the box, and find a gorgeous blue jeweled hair clip tucked inside. I pick it up, and Charlotte's murmured "Oh" fades into the background. It's lovely, and looks old. Intricate silver swirls cradle sparkling blue gemstones, in a pattern that reminds me of the swirling motions of deep water.

I look down and see a small note folded and resting on the cushion underneath. I set the beautiful clip back in the box, and open the note. It's scrawled in loose, manly script. *Why do men write in all capitals?* I muse before reading it.

Sadie,

Call me a romantic if you must, but this is my mother's. She wore it in her hair on her wedding day. If you're willing, I know it would thrill her if you'd wear it this afternoon. The day we met, I phoned her and asked if there was something she'd like to send me, and this is what she chose. She wanted me to tell you she can't wait to meet you, and that it's yours to keep as long as we share a last name. All that's left is to ask one of the girls to loan you something for the ceremony.

Can't wait to meet you at the altar,

Patrick

P.S. Check under the cushion

He called his mother the day we met? But that was before we were even matched, when I stumbled across him in the hallway! I hold the note tightly for a second, touched by his thoughtfulness in arranging this.

"What does it say?" Charlotte is on the edge of her seat, but I can tell she's tried very hard to let me have my moment. I pass her the note, and she lets out a gusty breath a moment later. "Oh my goodness gracious, does he have a brother? This is so romantic. The other girls are all going to be jealous!" She looks up, and I am just holding the clip, taking in all of the beautiful swirls.

"What's under the cushion?" her question snaps me out of my fascination, and I lift the edge of the cushion to see an antique silver coin. I lift it carefully and see the number 6 etched from the silver. She inches closer, and takes it in. "Oh, he's thought of everything! It's a sixpence, it's supposed to go in your shoe."

Hot cocoa, sentimental gifts, and a romantic at heart. It's official, I'm a goner. I tuck the gifts into my desk drawer, and spot the stack of letters for home I'd written last night.

"Charlotte, would you mind dropping these in the mail for me?"

"Of course not! I'll take those over this afternoon," she takes them with a gentle smile.

We make our way over to the bride's room to get our morning preparations underway. The sounds of Jenna's dance music is already pouring out. I poke my head around the doorframe, and see everyone except Margaret huddled in the room around Faith, who is smiling from ear to ear. Jenna is pinning up her hair, and Leigh is painting on some pink lip color.

"How's it going in here?" I ask, and Elena squeals.

"It's about time, girl! Get your short butt in this chair pronto! Where have you been?"

Charlotte answers before I have a chance, "Only being swept off her feet by Patrick."

Nell scolds me, "You're not supposed to see him until the wedding!"

I hold up both hands, "I didn't! He used Charlotte as his messenger."

Charlotte recounts the tale as Elena and Nell go to work on my hair and face. After multiple love-struck sighs, they all agree that Patrick gets major brownie points.

"You can pay him back later tonight!" Jenna cackles evilly, and I can feel myself blush the color of the leaves outside.

"Oh, leave her alone." Charlotte says lightly, and gives my shoulder a reassuring squeeze.

I shoot her a grateful look, but keep my reservations to myself. I know that most of the girls have already gone a lot further than the few kisses I've shared with Patrick, but I'm not comfortable taking things any faster than we have. Luckily, he seems okay taking it slowly, too.

The morning goes by in a blur of mascara and a cloud of hairspray. Elena finishes artfully arranging my thick chestnut hair into perfect curls, and fastens one side back with Patrick's mother's clip. A second round of oohs and ahhs erupt once that's on display. I hurriedly eat a few bites of lunch when it's delivered, and then it's time for me to put on my dress. It took me forever last night to choose, and I will never admit to a soul that I tried on every single dress they delivered in front of my full-length mirror. But when I saw this dress, I knew.

The full skirt was layer upon layer of gossamer tulle, topped with sparkling floral crystals that shimmered with every movement. The bodice hugged tightly up to my collarbone, continuing the floral pattern. The back, however, plunged low and open. It was both daring and classic, and it fit me like a glove. Not too fancy, not too plain. It was exactly the dress I didn't know I'd been imagining. Nell and Charlotte hold it up for me so I can step under, and then fasten the snap at the top which holds it together. I take off my fertility wristband, as today is the one day I'm allowed to remove it.

I rub absentmindedly at the spot on my wrist, and turn to see Faith's gorgeous crème gown. It's lacy and vintage, with a higher hem at her knees that falls away to the floor behind her. It suits her, and I think Teddy will be thrilled when he sees her. She smiles at me, and I smile back at her. It feels like a dream, that we're here, getting married together to people that we both actually like, and want to marry. The rest of the girls file out to put on their dresses, and Faith grabs our bouquets. Mine is a simple bundle of daisies, and hers is blush pink roses.

"Are you nervous?" she asks.

"A little," I admit, "I'm trying not to be. How about you?"

"No, not at all. I guess the benefit of the third time around is that you can see if a man is really genuine, or just telling you what you want to hear. If there's one thing I know about Teddy Taylor, it's that he's as genuine as they come."

"That's the truth. You sure that's a good thing?" I joke, trying to ease my own nerves.

"Absolutely. Come on, we're supposed to go wait in the back of the dining hall."

"Wait, I thought for the outdoor venue we were supposed to wait in the sports center. That's where I waited with Beth-Ann."

"Well, if we were getting married at the *usual* outdoor venue, you'd be right. But Teddy and Patrick have been sweet-talking the wedding-planning crew, and we've been given a special venue. Come on!" She walks out, knowing I'll follow.

Holding the bottom of my dress up so it doesn't get grass stained, I hurry after her. I breeze through the now-familiar courtyard without a second glance. We make our way into the very same hallway where Patrick led us to escape our kidnapping attempt. The memory reminds me that while this has turned out far better than I'd hoped, it's still not all rainbows and butterflies. I'm getting out of this with a man I won't mind taking home to my family when the time comes, but not without a cost to so many women.

I stand tall in the hallway, determined to do my part in fixing this broken system eventually. Faith is introspective as well, probably reliving her own memories of that night. A small eternity later, a familiar wedding planner pokes her head through the doorway.

"Hi, girls. I'm Melinda! Are you ready to meet your handsome grooms?" She has a twinkle in her eye, and you can tell she enjoys her job, regardless of the circumstances surrounding the weddings she plans.

"We are, Ms. Melinda. Lead the way!" Faith proclaims. She shuffles her bouquet into one hand, and reaches for mine with the other. I take her hand, and can't help but think that for someone without a sister of her own, Faith is really good at being mine when I need her.

We exit the door to find a long, freshly laid path of flower petals heading in the direction of the barn. The two of us follow Melinda, still hand-in-hand until we arrive at the stable yard. Right as we walk up, the traditional wedding march begins to play, and all of our new friends and their dates stand as we approach the aisle in the middle of the assembled chairs.

Rounding the hedges, I catch my first glimpse of Patrick and Teddy standing at the end of the aisle waiting for us. Faith lets out a breath, and switches our hands so we're linked at the elbow. Slowly, in time with the music, we make our way down the aisle. I can't take my eyes off of Patrick, and it feels like he's drinking me in. The smile on his face is slow, assured, and just so right. I feel like I'm walking on a cloud, as I make my way towards the new officiant standing with the men under a beautiful flower-bedecked arbor, right in front of the large barn entrance.

When we arrive, Faith gives me one last squeeze before letting go of my arm and reaching for Teddy's outstretched hands. I do the same, and Patrick's warm hold grounds me to this moment. The officiant begins the usual spiel, but I'm so lost in Patrick's beaming gaze that I don't hear a word until he says my name.

"Do you, Sadie, take Patrick to be your lawfully wedded husband?" he says.

"I do," I repeat quietly.

"Do you, Patrick, take Sadie to be your lawfully wedded wife?" he asks.

"I do," Patrick's voice is steady, resolute. He gives my fingers a squeeze, which I return.

We repeat more vows, promising to honor, cherish, and care for each other. To be partners in love and in life. The words are beautiful, and I find that I fervently hope the marriage promises we are making today we are able to keep, despite how hard the world is going to try to separate us. Deep down, I want that beautiful longevity that my parents have worked so hard to show me. I want that with Patrick.

Finally, the officiant says that the grooms may kiss their brides. Patrick slides one hand up my bare arm, and the other behind my neck. He leans in and brushes the softest of kisses against my lips, lingering there, begging to be deepened.

After a moment he pulls back a hair, and whispers, "Later," there against my lips. The look he gives me promises so much more when we're alone.

All of the girls and their dates stand and clap, as he announces us as new couples, and we make our way down the aisle. Right as we start down the aisle, Michael arrives at the end driving a white carriage pulled by none other than Twinkie and Doc.

I turn to Patrick in surprise, "Did you do this? This is amazing!" I walk to the front and give the boys scratches under the chin before letting him help me into the carriage across from Teddy and Faith.

"I thought you might like one last memory with the horses here before we have to go," he says with a shrug.

I can't help but throw my arms around him in a huge hug. "Thank you, Patrick. You've really thought of everything today." My hand floats up to touch the beautiful blue clip, and his eyes crinkle as he smiles.

"My parents will love you, Sadie. And my mom will be thrilled that you love the clip." He takes my hand in his.

Teddy breaks the mood by asking, "So, how long do we have to stick around at this reception before we get out of here?" while waggling his eyebrows exaggeratedly at Faith.

She whacks him on the arm, but laughs good naturedly.

"Hey, we may all be married now, but you keep that to yourself. I don't want any details, understand?" I give him my serious sister glare, and now it's his turn to laugh.

"You are too easy baby sister, you know that?" he says as he kicks my foot lightly under the edge of my gown.

I just roll my eyes in response.

Michael takes us on a slow loop around the property, and it's the perfect way to say goodbye to the beautiful grounds. He drops us off at the front entrance to the main hall, where everyone is waiting at the long central banquet table for our arrival.

They serve us delicious pasta ragù, which reminds me of my last date with Antonio, making pasta together. I make a mental note to try to make some for Patrick when we get to Mairmont.

The dinner flies by, and there is an abundance of laughter and good natured ribbing amongst the couples. It almost feels like we've all known each other for our whole lives, instead of just over a month. It's amazing how an experience like this, with all its ups and downs, can really bring a group together.

Talk starts to turn to who will be tying the knot next, with Hector making big eyes at Elena. Nell has really relaxed around Atlas, and it's nice to see her casually rest a hand on his forearm. She's filled out a bit since we've been here, and she looks much more at ease. Charlotte and Devonte are leaned in close to each other, whispering something. All in all, everyone remaining here seems happy, and that makes my heart light. Moments of unfettered joy are so rare; I breathe this one in to hold onto.

Dinner draws to an end, and a staff member lets us know that our shuttle is ready to take us to our honeymoon destination whenever we're ready. The four of us start to make our rounds, and we're given several promises to see us again soon in Mairmont. Patrick holds my hand through it all, and it's nice to have a partner for the next phase of this crazy path we're on.

We finally make it out to the hallway, and I can see the shuttle parked out front. There's Todd the driver, already loading up our collection of bags. Before we can make it out the door, though, someone in a uniform approaches us.

"I'm sorry to hold you up, but we need you in the program director's office for a moment to sign your marriage license," he says kindly.

"What about Faith and Teddy? They've already headed outside to the shuttle," I ask.

"Oh, they signed theirs separately this morning. If you'll follow me; it will only take a moment." He leads us off down a side hallway that I've never been down.

We arrive in a well-appointed office, and he holds the door for us. A man who I can only assume is the director is seated behind the desk, and he passes a folder with a single sheet of paper across to us with a pen. Patrick quickly signs, and then slides it over to me. I skim my eyes down the page looking for my name when I spot an issue.

"Uhm, excuse me. This is incorrect. The last name is O'Roarke." I point at the line, and slide the folder back across to the director for review.

He raises his eyebrows as he takes in the document. He looks to Patrick and says, "I'll give you two a moment." He stands abruptly and walks out of the office.

"Well, that was rude. Is he going to get us a new copy to sign?" I turn to Patrick, who is looking intently at the marriage license. I give him a playful poke with my elbow, "And what—are you in such a big hurry that you didn't notice they got your name wrong? It says right there Patrick . . . Royce."

He doesn't smile when he looks up at me, and my levity turns sour in the pit of my stomach.

"Sadie, there's something I need to tell you. My name is not Patrick O'Roarke."

TO BE CONTINUED

BEFORE YOU GO ...

Thank you so much for reading my debut novel, Dwindle! As a new author, it is so hard putting your first book out there for the world to see. You spending your time with my words is a true honor. I absolutely love to see your reviews and read your kind words!

Want updates on my latest releases and publishing process? You can sign up for my newsletter here: https://www.subscribepage.com/e0v1b5

Follow me on Facebook here: https://www.facebook.com/KAGandyAuthor

Or, email me any time: kagandyauthor@gmail.com

MORE BY K. A. GANDY

Bea Mine (Sweet Nothings Bake Shop, Book 1)

Love Makes you Stupid. Bea's too smart to fall into Cupid's trap. Or is she?

Bea is in love with George Anderson. No two ways about it, she has been since she was seven years old, and first met her bestie's older brother. When the pair is thrust together for a long Valentine's Day of bakery deliveries, can they resist the spark—and frosting—that flies between them?

HEA Guaranteed! Clean, sweet, and wholesome reads.

Will Travel for Love (Sweet Nothings Bake Shop, Book 2)

Bea and George hit it off, but Daphne's still a party of one. Will she find her forever traveling companion, or be alone in paradise?

Check out book two of the Sweet Nothings Bake Shop series, and see what Celia's got up her sleeve for Daphne. Or should we say, who she's got up her sleeve?

Dwindle (Populations Crumble, Book 1)

Torn from her home and family. Forced to marry a genetically matched stranger. Will she find love, or destruction?

Rise (Populations Crumble, Book 2)

The man she thought she knew truly is a stranger. Swept away on their honeymoon, the stakes have never been higher. Will his identity be their undoing, or will they rise together?

Reign (Populations Crumble, Book 3)

Kidnapped from their honeymoon resort, nothing is as it seems. Betrayal, intrigue, and secrets abound as Sadie works to free the captive women. But will she end up the savior, or the next captive?

Sweet Romance Anthology (Paperback Only)

A heartwarming and swoon-worthy collection of 26 sweet, romantic short stories.

ABOUT THE AUTHOR

K. A. Gandy was born and raised in Jacksonville, Florida, and is married with two kids. She has worked as a restaurant hostess, library book shelver, ranch hand, tour guide, Realtor, tech whiz, landlord, and small business consultant, all in addition to pursuing her passion for writing. As a person of many interests, her life has never been boring. She likes to write late in the evenings and thinks drinking hot tea and baking great cookies fuels hopes and dreams. If you would like to find more of her works, you can sign up for her newsletter at https://www.subscribepage.com/e0v1b5. You can also get updates on Facebook at https://www.facebook.com/KAGandyAuthor.